D1642936

Never Let Me Go...

Sachin Garg

GRAPEVINE INDIA

Grapevine India Publishers Pvt. Ltd.
Plot No. 4, First Floor,
Pandav Nagar,
Opposite Shadipur Metro Station,
Patel Nagar,
New Delhi - 110008
India
grapevineindiapublishers@gmail.com
contact@grapevineindia.in

First published in India by Grapevine India Publishers in 2012

Copyright © Sachin Garg, 2012

Typeset and layout design: A & D. Co.

To Mom

Acknowledgements

Writing this book wasn't really a solitary process and this is where I get to thank people who have helped me in the journey.

I have to thank Nikita Singh, possibly the most talented writer in the country at this time. People don't get to see the writing process of a writer, but if they did, the world would have known why she is the Sachin Tendulkar of the writing world. There is no doubt in my mind, that she would do really well in life.

In this book, she has hand-holded me, scolded me, overridden my suggestions, written parts of it and treated it with more love than some of her own projects. And most importantly, she has inspired a character, which I truly cherish. As this book goes in print, she could be more excited than I am.

Thank you, Nikita Singh, for being with me on this one. I hope I have thanked you enough.

Durjoy Datta, for having been with me on this joy ride of writing books. Come to think of it, it all started with one random thought on an idle afternoon.

Jayanta Bose, for being an ideal mentor.

Komal Rustagi, for her valuable inputs.

Naman Kapur, for being the mainstay of Grapevine India Publishers.

My three nieces, Rhea, Akshita, and one unnamed as of now, for smiling all the time.

Mom and Dad. For everything.

How to Get to WoodStock Village (Arambol)

Arambol is one of the northern most beaches in Goa. Tourists from India and abroad go there to spend time in a secluded environment, on a lonely beach.

WoodStock Village is a real place, which attracts an eclectic mix of people.

All other places mentioned in this book are real too.

Prologue

It was a bad summer. All I did was stay locked up in my room and stare at the ceiling. Mom was naturally worried about me and had decided to spend the summer in India, with me to see me through this summer.

I had a good reason to be messed up. But what really worried Mom was the fact that I was showing no signs of improvement. I was spending my days locked up in my room. I wasn't taking any calls from any of my friends. I wasn't eating properly. And Mom was at her wit's end to bring me back to normalcy.

The only time I got out of my room was when I went for my evening walk, every day. I needed some open sky and I had a well decided route for that. Sometimes, I used to stop by at a road side shop and have something from the shop. And at other times, I used to spot someone I knew and turn around and run until he was convincingly out of sight. I loathed conversations. In fact, I had lost interest in almost everything.

On the evening that I'm talking about, I sat idly in my room, like I did on most days. I felt a hand on my shoulder. I turned around to find Arshi, a very good friend of mine, who was getting equally annoying recently.

"So, how are you?" she asked, casually. But I knew that it was anything but casual. She had been pestering me with questions since a long while now. Arshi was a Psychology Honours student at Jesus & Mary College in Delhi. And she had a very annoying habit of applying what she read in books in real life. I knew that she meant well, but it was irritating nonetheless. She said she wanted to help me come out of the shell I had created around me after...

"I'm good. Can't be better," I said, forcing a smile, and trying to push away the images that had been haunting me 24X7.

Arshi was staring at me, as if she was analysing something very deeply.

"You're lying."

"No, no. I'm perfectly okay now. Tell me – how are you?"

"Cut the crap, Samar. You *have to* tell me," she persisted.

"You know what happened. What more do you need to know?"

"Yes, I know what happened. But I know there is more to the story. And I'm not letting go till you tell me all about it."

I was silent. Arshi had got it bang on. Apparently, she had been taking her psychology classes very seriously. But for me, she had brought back a storm of memories which I was trying to leave behind. My heart was a little too heavy for me to speak any further.

I was sure Arshi could see what was happening inside me. She could pick subtler hints. This was way too evident.

"You have to tell me everything, Samar," Arshi said. "I need to hear it from you."

"I can't do it," I said, breathing heavy now.

"You have to. You have to do it for yourself."

"But why?" I asked.

"Because you need to vent it out. You need treatment. You need to help me in helping you," she insisted.

I walked out of my room. There was no way I was going to live through everything again just to tell her the story. But when I saw my Mom sitting in the living room, I realized that it was a wrong decision to come out. Where it had been just Arshi breathing down my throat before, now it was Arshi and Mom, together.

I looked at their faces and realized that I was trapped. But I could not face it. After staring at Arshi angrily, I turned to leave the house.

"*Beta*, wait!" I heard Mom call.

"What?" I turned around and asked.

"Don't be angry at Arshi. I called her here," Mom said.

"What? Why?"

"Because I knew that she is the only person who can help you—"

"But I don't need any help! I'm perfectly alright!" I let out.

There was a short silence in the room. The looks on their faces said more than clearly that they were not buying any of it. I felt helpless. I had no way out. I could not afford facing all that again, to tell them all about it. The memories were terrible as it was. But I could not just walk out either. Mom had been worried about me ever since... And I knew I was being really mean to her all these days, as I sat locked up in my room. Mom deserved to know exactly what had happened. And Arshi didn't let go of anything she set her heart upon.

But it was way too painful for me to handle. I had to go away before they made me succumb to it.

"*Beta*, please... I've been worried about you..." Mom said in a low voice, just when I was about to leave.

And I knew I had lost the battle. I resented the tone of her voice; she was sad because of me. I took a deep breath in, as I realized what I had to do. I could not cause any more pain to her.

So yes, I began to tell the story of the twenty first year of my life. Definitely the most dreadful year there would ever be.

I Will Never Let You Go

Some couples go to bars and hang out. Some couples go to restaurants and have candle lit dinner. Some couples go to parks and find a lonely bench.

Kanika and I organized college events together.

Kanika lived in the college girl's hostel. The hostel rules didn't allow her to come out after eight. The only time when she could legitimately stay out after eight was when she was in the organizing team of some college event. So that's what we did. We organized one event after the other, to maximize the time we spent together. And once you are not a first year student, all it really takes is delivering instructions to an over enthusiastic Fresher for doing one thing or the other. Plus those extra two hours outside the hostel every evening – bliss.

We had organized all sorts of events. From Dr Stephan Pierre's guest lecture, Jasbir Jassi's celebrity night, Age of Empire's gaming competition, to the C++ programming thing, we had done it all. And it had all gone pretty smoothly, simply because we started working on the project way before schedule, so that Kanika could start staying out as soon as possible.

So the story really begins from my twentieth birthday. I had just entered the third year of my Engineering. And Kanika had just begun her second year. I was told that people now called us Samar-Kanika, as if we were one person, rather than two different souls. I didn't mind. Kanika, in fact, loved it.

The sad part about my twentieth birthday was that it was on the day of the Inter College Play Competition. It's not that I minded working on my birthday. But the sad part was that the Inter College Play thing was the last event of the season. With the end of this event, Kanika had no other excuse to stay out till late in the evening. Our evening good byes would be pre-poned by two hours. And it gave us a sinking feeling.

We were in the organizing team of the competition. Every day, we were the first ones to reach the auditorium, just because we used to be so excited to see each other. Today was no exception. I shaved my two day stubble and combed my very short hair. I had to bend a little because the room's mirror was adjusted for an average person's height. I was a good three inches taller than that. I looked at my dusky skin and I wondered what she liked in me. But as long as she did, I was not complaining.

I think I should tell you a little more about myself. I am Samar Garg, and am a typical guy. If you have heard a stupid typical habit that Delhi guys generally have, I probably have that. I live, look and walk Delhi. And yet, I am not very good at roads, just in case you were planning to call me next time you lose your way in the city.

I have received a total of 107 compliments for my looks in my life. That's right, I count. Because if you realize that out of those 107, I'd received 93 before the age of five, you'll realize that I don't get many. So it's an easy job to keep a count.

So yeah, I like to believe that I am tall, dark and awesome. And that works for me. Every night when I go to bed, I imagine the scar on the face of that guy I had seen on the railway station, or the villain of that Mithun movie, and thank my luck because I definitely look better than them.

In school, I used to be that geeky, creepy guy who sat on the last bench and solved engineering college entrance exam papers, instead of preparing for Class XII Board exams. When

I reached college, I became that guy who is somehow Kanika's boyfriend.

Also, I must tell you that my parents live in the Middle East. And I live with my roommate Roy, in an apartment, just outside my college in Delhi. It's a good life. I always say, twenty is a good age to be. All of you should be twenty, unless of course, you are not twenty.

Not digressing from the point, I made my way to the auditorium. I unlocked the door, entered and waited for her to walk in. When I heard her footsteps, my breathing rhythm got a little upset, as I braced for the visual. And when it did meet my eye, I felt something shift close to my spinal cord. It was as if little germs had shifted their space in that area, due to the utter excitement that the visual had caused in me.

She walked in, hugged me and wished me a Happy Birthday. We weren't very romantic like that. I guess our romance lied in the eagerness to be in each other's company all the time. We organized events together in our college and somehow, found comfort in that. It ensured that even though we were together for ten hours a day, we didn't get bored. It ensured that we always had things to talk about, topics to discuss, people to make fun of. It was the spice of our relationship.

Once the play started in the evening, both of us sat in a corner on the right side of the stage. Neither of us gave a rat's ass about what was happening on stage. We were busy catching up with each other, even after having spent almost every waking hour together in the last six months.

"So what do you want on your birthday, Samar?" she asked.

The area beside the stage was mostly dark, as the stage was primarily lit up with two spot lights. As we sat there, I looked at her and realized that I really didn't need anything.

"I am too much in love with you to want anything."

"But I want to give you something. How about... umm... a wallet?"

"But I don't want a wallet. Just let me kiss you right now, here in the dark, and that shall be enough," I said.

"C'mon. I know it's dark. But it's a little too open for us to be doing this."

"Nobody can see us. It's just a psychological barrier for you."

"Whatever it is, I can't do it," she said.

"Okay, then a wallet it will be. An expensive one."

"Guys, these days, have become so materialistic," she said and I saw the outline of her head move forward, to kiss me. I felt her breath on my upper lip. And just as her lips were about to touch mine, the play ended and the lights came on.

I got a full view of her face. And something in my chest shifted its place. My eyes were within a few inches of her midnight black, beautiful, huge eyes. I felt as if my eye lashes could touch hers, just like my breath which was mixing with hers. It was as if the turning on of the lights had given me such a high that even kissing might not have.

The visual high was no less.

Just then, I heard a sound. And I realized that we were sitting right where the actors exited from. And they had been looking at us, standing there all that while, ever since the lights had come on, thirty seconds ago. We looked at them, embarrassed. And then, we just got up and left the place before we died of embarrassment. We crossed the curtain and went where the audience was sitting. This was the best way to escape the embarrassment – by getting lost in the crowd, in the sea of faces.

We made sure that no one from that team saw us. We sat in the crowd until the last prize was given away and didn't go anywhere near the stage until that moment. And once it was done, we had to congratulate our production team for their phenomenal job, like every time.

Kanika spoke well to the team. When she spoke, people wanted to hear her speak. She was that sweet little girl, who wanted to keep everyone's interest in mind, in whatever she did, and at the same time, she was very sharp and knew how everything worked. She was a good leader to have.

I was standing right beside her and yet, I couldn't resist looking at her, unblinking. She looked unreal. Her flawless skin seemed to radiate light.

I know what you must be thinking. *That's what everybody says about the girl he is in love with. The girl is always breathtakingly pretty. So there is nothing new about these lines.* But the difference is – I am telling the truth. You should have seen her when she walked from her room to the hostel mess in her pyjamas. Right out of bed, with her hair all over the place. Her still-a-little-sleepy eyes, devoid of kohl would have literally taken your breath away. Not that I ever got to see her like that! She lived in a girls' hostel and I wasn't allowed in, but every morning, when I called her and she was making that call walk, I used to exhaust all my imagination to draw a mental picture of how she must be looking then. And that in itself was enough to make my day.

When she entered the class a little late, the first benchers took a deep breath, to smell her body wash. The lecturer stopped teaching to ask her why she was late, which was just an excuse to get a legitimate reason to look at her.

You might say that I am exaggerating. But this is how I saw it. And maybe, it really isn't about how it really was. It was more about how *I* saw it.

And for me – she was perfect. *We* were perfect. Life was blissful.

The Freshers wrapped up everything, leaving the auditorium, ready for us to call it a day. I was supposed to keep the keys to the auditorium for the night. Just as we lifted the final prop off the stage, Kanika announced like a high profile Bollywood director, 'Pack up!'

The Freshers ran out of the auditorium as if they had just won the First War of Independence against the British. And that, most fortunately, left Kanika and me alone in the auditorium.

"Let's go, then," I said.

Kanika didn't seem to like what I had just said. "Do we have to?" she asked softly.

"What other choice do we have?"

"It's your birthday…"

"So?" I asked.

"It's also the first anniversary of our first meeting. We had met for the first time on your last birthday, remember?"

"Yeah, I do." I actually did, I swear.

Kanika gave me a mischievous look. And then, she took out her phone from pocket and dialled a number.

"Hello, Mrs Sadhna? Hello, I am Kanika. I'm sorry for disturbing you so late. Yeah, I just wanted to tell you that something has just come up at my house. I am sorry; I will have to rush home right now. I am really sorry for bothering you at this hour. Yes, thanks. I sure will tell you when I am back. Okay, thanks, ma'am. Sure, I will get a letter signed by my dad when I come. Good night."

I heard Kanika lie smoothly to her hostel warden. The night's permission was taken care of. Usually, she didn't agree to night outs. She wasn't really a person who lied a lot. But that day was special and she knew we wouldn't be out together till late, for quite a few days, so she lied.

"I hope you can copy my dad's signature," she said, as she rubbed her shoulders to make herself feel warm. It wasn't all that cold outside but the air-conditioning in the auditorium was always overdone.

I took off my sweat shirt and gave it to her. She looked gorgeous in it. I didn't reply to her question. I just stepped forward and hugged her. "Have I told you recently, that I love you?"

I realized my mistake as soon as I said it. I mean – there are couples who say *I love you* with every full stop and comma in their sentence. And there are couples who don't say *I love you* for months, even though it is always hanging in the air, like the most obvious thing in the world. We were definitely the latter. In fact, I hadn't told her that I loved her for a long time, and asking the question that I just had, was something absolutely not recommended.

"You haven't told me that for a long time," she said.

"But I do," I said, still hugging her, her hair on my cheek, the smell of her shampoo completely in my head.

"You can do better. You're saying that after ages. Say it with style!" she said, as if she was throwing a challenge at me.

With a deep breath, I kind of accepted the challenge. I had never had a chance of being down on one knee in front of her before anyway.

So I held her hand and took her to the stage. We now stood where the spotlight had been, just a few hours ago. If there was an audience, we would have been in their full view right now. The acoustics of the room were such that even our whispers will echo in the whole auditorium. We were the hero and the heroine of the drama going on inside our heads.

We were standing in the middle of the stage of an auditorium, right where the spotlight must have been. I could not have had a better chance to do something really jazzy.

So I got down on one knee, and held her hand, just like I had seen in the movies. The only part left was opening my heart and pouring whatever I felt for her. And I started.

"In case you've been living on Mars for the last few months, I want to tell you my story. I've met someone. She is pretty and she smells... like home. You know what I mean? The way a bowl of Maggi reminds you of Mom, her smell reminds me of the comfort of my room, where I belong the most. Maybe it's the smell of her lip gloss or something.

It wasn't planned. I don't know if we were supposed to meet or not, but we have. She told me her name and where she was from. I told her that I suck at playing the guitar. She didn't seem to mind. And the next thing I knew in the middle of the fifth sentence coming out of my mouth, I wanted to spend the rest of my life with her.

And the girl is you, Kanika. That girl is you.

Today, this is finally happening; my being down on one knee moment has finally come.

I don't think anyone can know me as well as you do. It's not about knowing where I come from, or knowing what I would do when I am stuck in traffic or when the car tyre goes flat. It's not even about knowing all my stories. I think, in fact, it's about having been in all of them, there are things that we share which I can't ever do with anyone else.

And yet, when you will get to know me better still, you will realize how hard it is for me to actually tell you how deeply in love I am. Definitely, it is one of the hardest things I've done for you. And there's no easy way to do this. Except, baring my soul and telling you everything I've always wanted to say but they had seemed way too corny in my head.

I know you're tired of hearing this, but Kanika, you're beautiful. And I'm talking about physical beauty here. But the best part is – if I was to make a list of great things about you, physical beauty would probably be way down the list. Because you just keep giving me reasons to be blown away every single day, making me fall in love deeper and deeper.

And it's such a scary thought. I mean, come to think of it, this might be the most wonderful I might ever feel. This is the deepest love, anyone can ever experience. So many things can go wrong from here. But all I want to tell you is that I will try whatever I can to make it work."

It's a sin even if I try to put into words how I was feeling at that moment. I loved her and telling her made it only stronger. I felt good. It was blissful. She didn't say anything. I don't blame her. What do you say after a confession like that? I saw her eyes shine with unshed tears. I took her in my arms.

We went to the corner of the stage, her body touching my body as much as it could, we got down to the floor, and just lay in silence, savouring the moment, the feeling, the romance, and everything we had going on in our hearts.

We hugged in silence, and the best part was that there was nothing awkward about that silence. We loved every minute of it.

My lips started moving. I wanted to kiss her, but she moved her head back. I knew what she was doing. She was toying with me, pretending that she was not in the *mood* today. I knew her too well to be fooled by her pretence.

I decided to play along and test how long she could resist kissing me.

"Give me your phone," I said, and when she gave it to me, I told her that I was going to read her messages. Kanika hated it when I did that.

She grabbed for her phone but I moved my hand too fast. I straightened my hand in the air and challenged her to reach it. I was way too tall for her. As she jumped, her body rubbed against mine. It turned me on and I was sure, it had the same effect on her too. I looked at her, to check if she could resist the temptation of kissing me. She somehow was managing to resist herself.

I knew I would need to do something more.

"I need my wallet. It's in the pocket of the sweatshirt," I said, and extended my arm in to the sweatshirt's pocket. I came very close to her and my hands touched her body. With a friend, such a touch might have been very normal. But when you are standing alone in an auditorium with the love of your life, such a touch can send shivers of lust in your body.

This was it. There was no way Kanika could continue her little game. Her head moved forward and that was all she had to express. My head moved forward too. And we kissed.

Soon, we were down on the floor. When you make out with someone for the first time, there are set formulae and steps in making out. You start with a kiss and progress step by step to the next level of intimacy.

But Kanika and I had been together for a while. There were no steps. Our hands led the brain rather than the brain leading the hands. And there, right on the stage where the actors had walked in and out a little while ago, I made love to her.

"You are really good at this," I said, as I looked straight at her face without blinking.

"I read it up on the internet," she said.

"You read on the internet about how to be a good at making love?"

"Oh! You were talking about that?"

"Yeah. What did you think?" I asked.

"I thought you were complimenting my skin."

"That's good too."

"Thanks. But I got you right the first time itself. I do read on the net about that too," she said, as I bit her ear. We were lying on the floor, holding each other in our arms, not even clothes between the two of us. The joy of the moment was intoxicating.

"Samar?" she said.

"Yes?"

"Promise me that you will never let me go..."

I didn't reply. I just held her a little tighter, assuring her nonverbally that definitely, I will never let her go.

2

Made to the perfect fit

The next morning, I woke up hugging her. There are hugs which are awkward, which you indulge in, just because you are too sweet to take off her head from your arm. And then, there are hugs which are totally a part of you. It's as if her body has gelled into yours and yours has gelled into hers. As if both of you were made to be the perfect fit. Our hug was one of the latter. And it was one of the best parts of our relationship. We were so comfortable around each other. There was no pretending, no walking around eggshells, no faking. It was pure love.

We were in a corner of the stage, right where the actors must have climbed from, the day before. It was a good feeling to wake up to. Her hair was on my cheek. With her body as a pleasant weight in my lap, it was a morning I could live with, for the rest of my life.

She opened her eyes soon after and I looked into them. She gave nothing away, about what was going through her head. To somebody who didn't know her, they were just two plain black eyes with nothing behind them. But for me, every sight of them was her life story, which I knew better than anybody.

They told me of the passing away of her mom, only the year before, because of AIDS. I had been with her through that, along with some other friends. We had made it through and she had got back to a normal life, one way or the other. Her eyes told me of the years she had spent in Mumbai, learning her ways of life, which she unlearned when she joined my college, to learn new ways of Delhi. She was a year junior to me, and we had spent a year being in love. And I could see us spend a few more.

I know I was in love with her and hence my word doesn't count for much when I say this, but she was a good person to know. Everyone must know someone like her. She made you believe there was still goodness in the world. Good, genuine people still existed. And you could still trust people without thinking too much. She made you felt cared for, as if your existence and well-being really mattered to someone.

And when you looked deep into her eyes from a few inches away, you really thought that career, society, money, time, age, everything else in your life is just so pointless, when you can wake up to these eyes within a few inches of yours.

She broke the embrace a few minutes later. "I should go," she said, getting up.

"Go where?" I asked.

"To the hostel, where else?"

"What if I don't let you go?"

"I don't think you have a choice. I am still sleepy," she said.

"Come over to my flat. I promise I would clean it up before you enter."

"I don't sleep well in your flat."

"Then we won't sleep," I said.

"Then what will we do?"

"Order some pizza? Watch a movie?"

"And…?"

"Do some other things that you may like, too?" I winked.

"I guess I could come over for a little while."

We both knew what was in our heads. My flat was right opposite the college campus. So we were taking a morning walk from the auditorium to my flat. Small joys of life.

As we reached the flat, my lips were just waiting to land on her. I closed the door behind her, as she lunged onto me. Her weight was completely on me now. And her lips touched mine.

As the kiss entered the third minute, I heard the sound of a song being turned on. We turned around to see who it was. It was Roy, my roommate. He had his phone in one hand and he was making a video of our passionate kiss. In the other hand, he had a bottle of beer.

"C'mon, you two. You're doing great. C'mon, take some clothes off," he said, as Kanika and I now stood straight and looked at him.

"What are you doing, Roy?"

"I am making a video of you two. You guys just ignore me and get back to what you were doing. I'll get a good price for the video in Palika Bazaar."

"You'll sell this video in Palika Bazaar?"

"Yeah. If you take the top off, it's enough money for a month. If the pant goes off, then enough for a year," Roy said, as the two of us stood there, laughing.

Roy was that kind of a fellow. He had a joke for every occasion. Some other roommates could have killed the moment by getting all awkward on seeing his roommate glued to his girlfriend by his lips. Roy, instead, talked cheap and still looked cute. He was the biggest master of the art of cheap talking in the city.

"Roy, are you drinking at seven in the morning?" Kanika said, pointing at the bottle of beer in his hand.

"Yeah, I was hung over from the drinking last night. So thought, a drink might help."

"No wonder you look two months pregnant!" I said, pointing at Roy's beer belly.

Roy shoved the thought away, as he took back his seat on the sofa and put the laptop back in his lap and got back to what he had been doing before we had come in.

"What are you doing, Roy?" Kanika asked, trying to change the topic.

"I was just spending some time on Facebook, stalking girls I am never going to get."

"Aren't you doing that every time I come to this flat?" Kanika asked.

Roy smiled, because that could have easily been the truth. "Yeah, I know I do that a lot. You know what my ultimate dream is?"

"What?"

"That I have thousands of pretty girls in my friend list."

Kanika looked at his computer screen. He was at 137 friends at the moment. And like most engineering college students, he mustn't have had any girls amongst those too. Kanika looked at his plump display picture.

"Well, I could tell you where to start," Kanika said.

"Where?"

"Start from the gym. And stop drinking beer. I assure you results within a year," Kanika said, as the two of us entered my room.

It was early morning. Neither of us had slept well the previous night but sleep was the last thing on our mind. I kissed her, as we went into the room and took off all our clothes.

We slept soon after and woke up a few hours later by the sound of some metal being kept on the floor. Kanika and I looked at each other, wondering what the sound was.

Kanika got out of the bed and into her clothes, as I looked on. And we came out of the room to find Roy standing outside, just in his boxers, with a dumbbell each in his hand. On seeing Kanika, he got startled and lunged for his T-shirt kept on the chair nearby and wrapped it around his boxers. It was a funny sight.

"What are you doing?" Kanika asked, in between laughing the loudest laugh my flat had heard in recent times.

Roy didn't bother to answer. Instead he dashed to his room, only to come back a while later, dressed in his pyjamas. The T-shirt around his boxers was now on his body. He had a glass of milk in his hand.

"Why didn't you tell me she was still here?" Roy said, looking at me. He was all red in the face. I was still trying to control laughter.

"Oh my God! Roy, are you having milk?" Kanika asked.

"Yeah. I thought it is time I quit drinking and lived in a healthy manner."

"So you'll quit beer?"

"Yeah. And I thought I'll start working out," Roy answered.

"You can never impress girls, Roy," I said.

"I knew you would say that. But it's all going to change. Three months in the gym and I will have a body to die for! I've figured out what girls want. I am going to hit the gym every day from now onwards."

"C'mon, Roy. Girls do want a lot more than just muscles," Kanika said.

"Like what?"

"Some personality. A good voice. And in some cases, a good face," I said.

"Exactly my point," Roy said.

"Your point?"

"See, I can't do anything about my voice or my face. But I can do something about my body. So I am just working on that!"

Kanika laughed out loud on hearing that.

This was typical Roy. He had a single point agenda for being on earth – getting laid. He ate, slept, and drank thinking women. And yet, at twenty, he was as much a virgin as he was born. And the struggle to get laid had thrown him into frenzy, a frenzy of thinking newer and better ways to attract women. He had tried everything. The latest cosmetics, borrowed cars, fake accents. But nothing seemed to have worked till now.

But he wasn't that bad either. With his good conversation skills and *in-your-face* smartness, he was a transformation waiting to happen.

"So you think it will work?" I asked.

"Yeah, I just need to be introduced to some girls now. Kanika, don't you have any hot friends you could hook me up with?" he asked.

"Well, let me think... I could hook you up with Maansi?" Kanika suggested.

"Maansi? I like the name. Tell me about her."

"What do you want to know?" Kanika asked.

"Is she horny? How big are those?" Roy asked, pointing to his chest area.

Kanika looked at him. "You know what, Roy? For a second, I thought maybe hooking you up won't be that bad an idea. But when this is the first question you ask about a person, it really gives me second thoughts." That was almost as rude as she could ever be. She was too sweet to say more.

"Is that a *yes*?" Roy asked.

"From where I see it, that is nothing but a *fuck off*," I said, laughing.

"Shit. Give me another shot. I promise I will ask a good question now," Roy said.

"Okay," Kanika said.

"What kind of guys does she like?"

"Oh. Well, let me think. Maansi is class personified. So naturally she likes classy, polished boys who genuinely have good lineage. I mean she radiates sophistication wherever she goes."

Roy's little hope had vanished already. This girl had out-of-league plastered all over her.

"What else?" he asked in a meek voice.

"Well, also, I think she is more into intellectual guys. Guys who exude smartness or something."

Roy nodded and thought long and hard about it.

"Still, talk to her and let me know what she thinks. For all you know, something might work."

"Hmm," Kanika said, not committing. I knew what must have been going through her mind. She must have been wondering if Roy deserved a chance with her friend.

"So what plans for the day?" I asked Kanika.

"I have to go back to the hostel by eight, and it is six already."

"We so need to find another event to be organized together so that you can stay out till late."

"Yeah. But for now, I have a very romantic plan," she said.

"I am listening."

"Let's visit the doctor together today," Kanika said.

"Why will we go to the doctor?"

"My asthma is causing some problem. I want to meet the ENT specialist."

Kanika had had asthma since she was a kid. But it had gotten worse since her mother died. Ever since the time Radhika Aunty died, Kanika's health had started to deteriorate too. And though she subsequently recovered from most of it, the asthma was something that didn't better with time.

I was getting worried about her. She had had two asthma attacks in the last eight months. Though the condition was mostly under control, she still needed to be on medication all the time. And the visits to the doctor had become a more regular affair.

So that's what we did that evening. We visited the doctor. And it should have been boring, but since we were together, it was anything but that. It was fun. When we sat in the waiting room, we made fun of all the photos in the magazines. When we were inside with the doctor, I couldn't stop laughing at the expression on his face when he peeked into Kanika's throat. Kanika joined me in the laughter, when he looked away.

Just then, the doctor got a call.

"Give him one unit of blood, until I reach. I know it is a critical case but there must be at least one unit of blood in the blood bank. Are you kidding me? You don't even have one unit?" we heard the doctor shout into the phone.

"What blood group are we talking about?" I asked the doctor softly.

"B+."

Neither of us had B+ blood group. But I knew that Roy did.

So I asked Kanika to call him up and tell him to reach the hospital address given by the Doctor.

Kanika explained the situation to him. But Roy was in a naughty mood.

"What do I get in exchange?" Roy asked Kanika naughtily.

"You are getting nothing in exchange for this. Goddammit, it's a serious thing, Roy!"

"But I do need something in exchange. Otherwise I am not moving an inch."

"What?"

"You will make Maansi accept my Friend Request on Facebook," Roy said, smiling on the phone.

"Okay! I will! Now run!" Kanika said.

"Relax. I'm already halfway to the hospital. I had left home the moment you gave me the Hospital's address," Roy said and hung up.

Kanika looked at me and suddenly her tensed expression changed into a smile. I knew Roy must have done another one of his cute stupidities.

And when everything had settled, Kanika and I looked at each other. We were both thinking the same thing. Actually, it was more of Kanika's idea. Ever since her mother passed away, she had been doing her bit for AIDS and cancer patients. I remember times when she put in a few hundred rupee notes in the transparent boxes they keep at various shops for collecting money for AIDS and cancer patients. Yes, she is a kind soul behind her tough, headstrong exterior. We reached my flat and turned on my laptop, and together, we started working on the poster for the Blood Donation Camp we would be organizing together.

She was excited about helping people; I was excited about helping myself. It was the next event to be organized by Samar & Kanika.

3

In spite of Because of the imperfection

It was one of those nights when Kanika and I had talked through the night. It's amazing how we still find so many things to talk about. Anyway, I had just disconnected the call, when I saw Roy still awake and working on his laptop.

"Hey, what's up?" I said, walking in.

"Nothing," he said and hid his laptop screen.

"Porn?"

"Umm… I was just photo-shopping my pictures to upload them on Facebook," he said.

"What? Show me?"

"It's nothing to see! Just touching up my pictures a little bit."

"But *why*?" I asked.

"It's more important to have a good display picture on Facebook than being good looking in real," he said.

"Are you serious?" I said, and bent forward to see what he had done to his picture. I was shocked on what I saw. He looked twenty shades fairer, with clearer skin, and an aberration on his cheek now looked like a dimple.

"I didn't know you had a dimple."

"I don't have it, but with the right functions in Photoshop, I can conjure an illusion of a dimple on my cheek. Girls love dimples, man," he said.

"Whatever!" I shrugged.

"So, today, when Maansi will accept my Friend Request, she will see a dimple smiling straight through her," he said. I wanted to tell him she was more likely to see the layers of double chin above his neck. But I chose not to burst his bubble. Instead, I started getting ready for the eight thirty lecture.

Kanika and I had ended up being inseparable. Luckily, that year, the professor were not giving students a hard time, so we ended up spending a lot of time together. And now that we had a Blood Donation Camp to organize, we were back to spending those extra two hours in the evening together, putting the posters and the flex in the right place.

That evening, as I was putting the bed in the right place, and as Kanika arranged the syringes and the needles, Roy called.

"Samar, where are you?" he said, in an unnaturally excited voice.

"Auditorium, why?"

He disconnected the call and ten minutes later, he was in the auditorium.

"So, what's the news?" Kanika asked him.

"Maansi accepted my friend request and I liked all her pictures and left flattering comments on all of them. But, guess what?"

"What?"

"Maansi Ahuja likes your photo. MY PHOTO!" Roy said, as if he was about to tear up out of joy.

"She liked one picture of you. Big deal," I said, not realizing the importance of it.

"Oh, that's not where it ended. This is the good part. I waited all afternoon for her to come online, so that we could chat. And when we did, it was so awesome."

"Why? What did she say?"

"It's not about what she said! It just that – she is so cool. The best sense of humour. Such wit. I'm so madly in love."

"She is a really good friend of mine, so please don't do anything stupid," Kanika said.

"Why would I do that? And we are chatting at twelve again today."

"Not bad at all," Kanika said.

"You think so?"

"Yeah. Just don't... I mean... please be nice to her. She's a good girl," Kanika said, as she entered her hostel gate and said bye to us.

Kanika had mentioned Maansi to me a few times before this. She had said that Maansi reeked of money and sophistication. They used to go shopping together and Kanika respected Maansi for her impeccable taste in clothes. Though not drop dead gorgeous, Kanika had told me that she was pretty and had really sharp features.

"So, you seriously fancy a chance?" I asked Roy.

He looked at me and shrugged. He still didn't know. But from what I had heard about Maansi from Kanika, I thought his chances were very bleak. But still, I wanted him to keep trying with all his heart.

"But it feels so good," Roy said, as we walked towards our flat. That was a completely new side of Roy I was seeing.

A 'what?' escaped my mouth.

"I mean – all these months, I used to see you and be jealous on seeing your perfect life. And now, I am myself in love with a real girl. I just love the feeling."

I didn't say anything. But my reaction must have given it away. Roy figured that maybe, it wasn't all rosy being in love.

"What? You're not happy with your relationship?" he asked.

"I sure am. But I just want to tell you that there are downsides too."

"Like?"

"Leave it," I said.

"You think I am going to let it go?"

Somehow, he managed to get me started.

I told him that first of all, you have to close your eyes to all the other beauties around you, which is difficult enough. And second, you have to ignore all her shortcomings and love her the way she is. I didn't mind the first part at all because frankly, there weren't many girls who made me feel like looking at them with Kanika at my side. But I did struggle with the second point every now and then.

Like this one morning, I had woken up after a really nice dream and was feeling really happy and all. So when I went to college and saw her, I hugged her instinctively. It was an impulse action.

"Stop overdoing the affection," I was smacked with.

I never instinctively hugged her again. And then, one fine day, when we were casually having coffee in a coffee place, she looked a little off. When I asked her why, I was bombarded with "You don't love me anymore. You don't even hug me for no reason like you used to."

I had no idea what I was supposed to do. I was blamed for something or the other no matter what.

When she went shopping, I used to pick her bags and go wherever she went. If I didn't come along, I at least had to pick and drop her. If I refused, I was bombarded with "Don't I come for shopping when you go?" What she doesn't mention is that I take ten minutes to shop, while she takes a whole day. And even then, there will be things she forgot and there will be plans for another spree next week.

And add to that – getting that stuff changed in two more visits. And then the crib about what she didn't buy.

When she would call, if I say 'I am busy', all hell would break loose. She would coax you into talking 'just for a minute'.

And then, when you wouldn't have stuff to talk about, hell will break loose some more. "You are shutting me out. You don't even tell me what's going on in your life. Are you hiding something from me?"

And you know what the worst part is?

That after reading this if you could go and talk to her, it will take her a minute to convince you that it is me who is pure evil in the relationship.

Phew.

Okay, not distracting from the topic. In spite of all this, I was definitely, madly in love with her. Despite these minor glitches, there was no other girl I ever wanted. For me, she was the only one that mattered. And slowly, I had come to love her imperfections too. I was truly crazy about her.

As I was done with my rant, we had reached our flat. I was supposed to go to sleep, and he was supposed to catch Maansi for a chat at twelve. He seemed happy. I was content. It was a happy flat we were living in, though I had no idea that Roy's happiness would turn out to be an eye sore to me the very next morning.

I woke up at my usual time, at eight fifteen for the eight thirty lecture. With a brush deeply ensconced in my mouth, I trudged to Roy's room to see him on his study table. My eyes popped out as the only purpose that the study table served was to dump used clothes. This was different.

"What the..." I said. "You are still awake?"

"I haven't slept," he said. "And now, you're going to help me."

"Help you? In what?"

"Did Kanika tell you that Maansi is into the whole Spirit of

Living business? Gurus and what not? Okay, whatever. The thing is that she organized a seminar in her college and her Guru is coming. So, last night, she was struggling to write an opening introduction piece. I had offered to help her out, but it's been four hours and all I have written is crap. You've got to write it for me, man."

"And why should I?" I asked, still brushing.

"Because you are my roommate. And roommates help each other to get the girls they love!"

"How will you *get* her by writing this?"

"Well, I told her that I would need a treat if write this for her. And she said, yes!" Roy said, cheerfully.

"She did?"

"Yes. So now, it's all in your hands Samar." He looked at me with sympathetic eyes.

"Sorry, man. I have a class to go to."

"Please."

"Fuck you," I said and went back to my room.

He followed me till I banged the door on his face. And when I came out, all dressed up for college, he was still there.

"I'm getting late for the class," I said.

"And you would have to miss this class for me."

"Aren't you stretching your luck a bit too much, Roy?"

"It will hardly take you ten minutes!" he pleaded desperately.

"Alright. I'm out of here," I said, and dashed for the door, but Roy reached the door before me and blocked the door with his arms. He had that look in his eyes. He was serious. I knew I had no way out. I had to give in. I skipped the lecture and went through the charade, complaining too much while writing the introduction. I picked most portions from what he had written, and he wrote brilliantly well, and made it into a nice doable piece. But I didn't let go of the chance of telling him that he owed me one, big time. Roy had boasted that he would be able to get it done by ten and that it was no big deal.

And his paranoia as the clock neared ten was freaking me out. From the moment he clicked on the sent tab on his mail account, instead of smoothing out, he got even more paranoid.

And then, the two of us stared for a reply to come. There was none.

"Why is she not replying? Did she hate what I wrote? Obviously she did. And now she is too shy to tell me that it was stupid. Oh my God, I should have never listened to you Samar."

"She hasn't replied because normal people are in college at ten in the morning, asshole." I shut him up. "And now, if you would excuse me, I have to attend some classes too," I said and left my flat. Never before had I looked forward so much to attending a class. That was some relief.

Roy came to the lecture hall only after lunch. It was evident that he was exceptionally happy.

"What happened?" I asked, as he sat next to me in the lecture hall.

He just grinned madly and said nothing.

"Will you tell me what happened?" I asked.

"She liked what I had written. So, she now has to treat me. Amazing, isn't it?"

"Wow! So when are you meeting her?"

"I told her that I'll be out of town for two weeks and would meet her only after coming back," he said.

"Why would you do that?"

"Because meeting her is going to need preparations."

"What kind of preparations are we talking about here?" I asked.

"I browsed through her albums and she looks fucking rich, Samar. All guys around her wear expensive-looking clothes and have big cars and shit. We can't do anything about the second part, but I can get the first part right at least?" he asked, in all seriousness.

"And how exactly?"

"Don't worry, I have figured out everything."

"Oh, no," I said. I knew that we were in deep trouble.

It took a little effort, but we finally managed to get everything Roy needed to impress his date. And everything we arranged was from the labels we had always loved, but could never afford. How we managed all that is a story we shall keep for some other time, but it cantered around borrowing books from seniors and selling them off. Anyway the point is that Roy, after a lot of hard work, was well prepared for his first date – New clothes, new shoes, same old attitude.

The date with Maansi was like the round two of Roy's life. It was as if no matter whether it went well or not, Roy would never be the same person again after this date. He would either start loving himself or the contrary. Either way, he was looking at it as a huge event. Add to that the fact that he had almost invested two complete weeks in preparing for this one, much more than he had ever invested on any tennis tournament or important exam, the stakes were definitely high.

On the evening when he was finally scheduled to meet her, he shaved his stubble, leaving only the goatee, like a well maintained undergrowth. He half combed his hair and took the price tags off the shoes and the shirt and slipped into them.

He was right. He had successfully managed to look like a different person that day. I felt a little proud of him. I had not given him much of a chance. But now, he seemed to demand it. He had prepared well.

I extended my hand to wish him the very best for the evening.

4

The Big Date

Roy came back earlier and happier than I had expected. I was on the phone with Kanika when he came back. We were waiting to hear how it had gone.

"Hey, Roy is here," I told Kanika.

"You guys talk, then. I will hit the sack," she said.

"Okay, goodnight then."

"Goodnight. Love you," she said, in her strikingly sweet voice.

I turned to Roy, to hear his story. After all the work we had put in getting him prepared for the date, I was really excited to know how it went.

"So, how was it?" I asked.

"Well actually, I have no idea how it was. She could have liked me, or it could be that she was just being nice. I have no idea. She did laugh at my jokes. But she could be acting, right? But why would she fake? I don't know, really. Fuck."

"Oh, whatever. But are you guys meeting again? What did she say about that?"

"It was something like – *I will definitely see you. But I won't tell you whether I am looking forward to it or is it because I am too impolite to not meet anyone again,*" Roy said.

"So you mean to say that she was mysterious?"

"Not really. Just that she is just so proper and fucking high-class that you can't deduce anything from her reactions."

"Hmm. So I guess, we are left with just one way of finding out what she thought of you...?" I said.

"Really? What?"

"Kanika. Who else?"

Somehow, Roy had not thought of that. Kanika and Maansi were old friends. They were supposed to tell everything to each other, right? I called up Kanika but she didn't pick up my call. I wasn't surprised. She must have slept off. I should have expected that.

"Why don't you message Maansi?" I suggested.

"Are you crazy? How can I message her without knowing whether she liked me or not."

"Hmmm."

And hence began a nervous wait for the morning, for Roy. I could see it in his body language. He really wanted this girl. And yet, in this night, there was nothing he could do about it.

The next morning, I got up at my normal time, fifteen minutes before the eight thirty class. And I finally saw the sight, I had thought, I would never get to see on waking up. Roy had taken a shower, slipped into a neat checked shirt and combed his hair already. I had never seen him look forward to college so much. He made me get up, and get ready in a jiffy. But the first class of the day was not what he was concerned about. He made me call Kanika and ask her to meet us.

We reached the college in time, thankfully, because by the time we met Kanika, Roy was almost hyperventilating and it looked like he would pass out.

"Well..." Kanika started telling us, what she had been told. "I could make out that she definitely did not hate you. She must have liked some things about you for sure. Just that..."

"Just what?"

"Just that you were almost there but still not there. It was as if you had everything but just not something."

I turned to Roy to see his face. I had never seen him so despondent. He had always been that lively guy everyone turned to when they needed some nonsense to light up their lives.

"You have any idea what it could be?" Roy asked Kanika.

"Well, knowing Maansi for so long, I just think you should do something which makes her believe that you are somebody... I mean like, somebody who is serious about his life. Not just a regular, aimless college student. See, Maansi's last boyfriend was an IITian who is now working in Deustche Bank in Germany, drawing a salary with a million zeroes. The one prior to that was a national level squash player. I don't want to disappoint you, but she has always had boyfriends like that and she is kind of spoilt for choice. She likes passionate, serious and successful men. "

"Hmm. But I am very serious about life," Roy said with a straight face but broke into a smile soon after.

"That's what I think about her. I could be wrong," she said, sounding a little apologetic. She knew the date meant a lot to Roy.

The moment Roy was back to his goofy self. It was good to see him back like that. Having a friend crying for a girl is not fun at all. But my joy was short-lived.

5

Born For It

Twenty is a good age to be. All you have to worry about is some stupid assignments and a set of exam here and there. One is still pretty shielded from the unpleasant topics like bosses, salaries, career etc.

Marriage was an alien concept which happened to elder brothers and sisters of friends. So when I got to know that my friend Zeeshan had suddenly planned to get married to my friend Arshi, I was definitely taken aback. Kanika was the one to have made them meet. They had always seemed so perfect for each other. Both of them, having done their share of falling for the wrong people, decided to get settled by getting married.

Zeeshan and I were unlikely friends. He came from the second world of Indian guys. I mean the first world is of course of that of Engineers, the one that I belong to. The second world of Doctors, which Zeeshan belonged to. But his life hadn't shaped the way most doctors' lives are. He had left the medical profession far behind. Instead, he had devoted his life to the art of playing the guitar. He was a good six or seven years elder to me. But because of his good looks, he didn't look strange when he stood beside me.

Arshi and I, on the other hand, went back a long time. We were friends from the neighbourhood and we had had our share of ups and downs. She was as old as me, but when she met Zeeshan, she knew he was the one for him. She didn't mind getting married so early.

But that's not the point. The point is that two people from my friend circle were actually getting engaged! It was a scary thought. I was sure the next time the topic of marriage will be touched with my Mom, she would definitely mention the two of them. The entire feeling of getting married and then, not being available for hanging out with buddies, forget getting drunk. And then progressing on to the concept of having babies. Unthinkable!

I was happy being a kid, just out of my teens.

On the day of the wedding, Kanika had left for the venue at two in the afternoon. She was supposed to accompany Arshi in the whole getting ready business. That meant she would be getting ready alongside the bride. All throughout the evening, I kept thinking of how she would look. I reached the venue at eight but Kanika was supposed to enter only alongside Arshi. I was so restless that I could not even concentrate on the gol-gappas in my hand.

And then she entered. She looked like a sari model, walking some ramp in some reputed Fashion Week. If you were meeting her for the first time, you could miss her make up easily. That was the thing about her dressing up. She was elegant and definitely not overdone. Her hair was tied at the back. Her eyes and lashes were made up. Her cheeks were shining. She looked amazing.

I looked at Zeeshan, sitting on the groom's couch, trying very hard to look happy. For most people, he must have almost pulled it off. But having known him for some time now, it was very obvious for me that he wasn't very sure which circus he was in.

"So how does it feel?" I asked Zeeshan as I approached him, because this was the only question playing on my head all this while.

"What do you think? Obviously it feels like shit!"

"Cheer up, man. Honestly, I had expected you to be happier today," Roy added.

"Well, I was happy till yesterday. But then..."

"Then?"

"I had never officially proposed her. You know, like getting down on the knees or say something sweet. She just texted me that it is her life-long dream that somebody does that for her..."

"Can't you do it now?" I asked, barely suppressing a smile at Arshi's stupid *dream*.

"But she wants a proposal. She just asked me send her a text and I have no idea what to write. Why can't she just concentrate on the getting married part?" he asked, exasperated.

"Why don't you send her one?" Roy asked.

"Dude, I am getting married. I am already nervous. I can't write anything right now."

"Never mind, Roy will write one for you! He just fell in love, I am sure he can write," I joked and laughed out at my own joke.

"Are you serious?" Zeeshan asked. He had taken it seriously. How was I to know that even Roy had?

"Yeah, I'll be back," Roy said and left the stage, where we had been sitting. I saw Roy go towards the food counter and dig into his mobile phone. He was typing frantically in his phone. He kept writing for a good one hour. I had never seen him so deeply engrossed in concentration for one full hour, not even in an exam. He was doing it with his whole heart.

"Is he any good?" Zeeshan whispered in my ear.

"I think so. And it's better than sending a blank text, isn't it?" I said, and Zeeshan nodded.

A little later, he sent the message to Zeeshan and came up to us. "Do you like it?"

It was Zeeshan's turn to be engrossed in his mobile, as he read what Roy had sent. He read and then he looked at me. And I knew what he was going to say next from his expression. He loved what Roy had written.

"It's AWESOME!" Zeeshan almost shrieked out. "You should do this for a living man!"

He almost hugged Roy! We waited while Zeeshan hit the

send button. We waited for a reply. Twenty minutes passed by and there was no reply.

"Maybe, she doesn't have her cell phone with her," Zeeshan said, nervously.

And just as he said that, his phone beeped and it was text from Arshi. We all peered into the cell phone.

Now, I know that getting married to you the best thing I have ever decided to do. Tears.

Your wife,

Forever and always.

:'(

Zeeshan, this time couldn't resist and hugged Roy. He almost had tears in his eyes. That text from Arshi meant a lot. Just then, his phone started ringing and it was Arshi. We walked away from him to give him some privacy.

Just as we started eating, we saw Kanika walk towards us.

"Zeeshan is so sweet," Kanika said.

"Why?" I asked.

"Arshi was crying and I asked what happened. She showed me a text that Zeeshan had sent her. She didn't let me read the whole of it, but I nearly had tears in my eyes too. They are such a sweet couple."

"Tears? In your eyes? Man, I am good!" Roy said, his chest filled up with pride.

"*Excuse me?*" Kanika said and Roy thrust his cell phone in her face and showed her the text in the sent items. Kanika and I read the text together. We finished reading the text and we were shocked.

Just then, Arshi came out and walked up to the stage. Not everybody must have seen it but I saw her hand move and hold Zeeshan's hand for a second, assuring him everything was okay now. There was love in their eyes. Roy's words had done the magic.

I turned around and looked at Roy.

"You wrote it?" Kanika asked, shocked.

"Your words can make people fall in love," I said to him.

"Yeah, they really do," Kanika agreed.

Roy looked at both of us. And then, he gave us a blank look, as if something revolutionary was going through his head. And the very next moment, he turned on his heel and left the engagement party. Kanika and I had no idea what had gotten into him all of a sudden. We just watched as he ran from the hall.

Roy stopped running only when he had reached the flat. He reached the room and threw his coat on the sofa and tie on the chair in his room. He picked out his laptop. He turned on Microsoft Word, and started writing his very first novel.

This was it. This was his big idea. He would write a book, even though he had no background in writing. Until very recently, he didn't even know he could write any better than a normal guy. He was an Engineer. But when he is bitten by a bug, he has to do something about it. This, he believed, would fix everything the way he had wanted. Roy wrote through the night. When he sat down to write, he checked that it was 10 PM. The next time he looked away from his monitor, it was 7 AM. He had been writing for the last nine hours, without even a single toilet break. This was his true calling. He now knew what he had been born for.

Once Roy had left Zeeshan's engagement party, Kanika and I were suddenly left alone. We had the food, which was pretty good and waited for an appropriate time to leave. Just then, Kanika began to have some breathing problems.

"Are you alright?" I asked.

"I can't... breathe..." she said, almost choking.

"You have some medicine?"

"Yeah... my tablet... in my purse..."

I opened her purse and frantically looked for the tablet. I

motioned a waiter to quickly get a glass of water.

"Here, take it," I handed over the tablet, with the glass of water. Once she had taken it, I motioned her to leave.

"Where are you taking me?"

"You need to see a doctor!" I said.

"No, no. I am okay. I need to be with Arshi."

"Are you crazy? You *really* need a doctor."

Kanika gave me that look. An assuring, *I-have-it-in-control* kind of look. I wasn't left with any argument. But it definitely was a scary incident.

Once things did wrap up, it was finally time for us to make a move. It had been a tiring evening. I was looking forward to my bed. I was supposed to drop Kanika to Arshi's place, where she would stay for the night.

"Thanks, Samar," Kanika said, for no apparent reason.

"What for?"

"For getting so paranoid when I'm unwell. For being so tensed when you called the waiter for water."

"It was scary to see you like that."

"I know. But it's good to know that there's someone who will take care of me when I would look scary."

"Obviously there is," I said, holding her hand, reassuringly.

There was a brief silence in the car. My thoughts started wandering and I was sure, so were Kanika's.

"Arshi looked really happy today," Kanika said. That told me which way her thoughts had wandered.

"Yeah."

And there was another pause. But this time, my thoughts couldn't wander. I was busy thinking which way Kanika's thoughts were going. And I had a very bad feeling that she was thinking about the concept of marriage. Basically, I didn't have an opinion on the concept of marriage. The only opinion I had was that it was too early for us to be touching this topic, even though both of us knew we were with each other forever.

But the tension might have showed on my face.

"What is wrong, Samar?"

"What? No, nothing?"

"Oh, okay."

When a woman says 'oh okay', it is anything but 'okay.' It means you should run.

"So where are we headed?" Kanika asked. "I mean… our relationship. Where is it headed?"

Just what I had feared all evening, having to 'talk'. "I haven't really thought about it," I said.

"One year into the relationship and you haven't thought where this is headed?"

I was dumbfounded. This is the moment every guy starts dreading once he tells a girl that he loves her. That someday, he would be standing face to face with the girl and she would ask him where all this is headed.

She continued, "See, I am not saying I want you to marry me tomorrow. I am not saying you have to promise me that you will marry me someday, whenever it will be," she said.

She was setting the ground for big bouncer.

"But I want to have hope Samar. I want to believe we are up to something. That all this is headed somewhere."

I looked at her. There was genuine concern in her eyes. And that concern translated into an innocence which no one can ever fake. That moment reminded me why I was so deeply in love with her. We were sitting in a car and had I not been driving, I would have hugged her then. The moment definitely deserved it.

"Isn't it enough that I truly love you?" I said.

I didn't have her innocent eyes. But I had said it with great intensity, assuring her that I could not mean more than what I was saying right now. And yet, it seemed to have failed to pierce her. It was as if she didn't buy my promise and I didn't stir any emotion inside her. After dropping Kanika, I came to my flat and slept off.

6
Contended

Life in the third year went on. Professors tried hard to screw our lives. But they didn't really exist for us. An assignment here, a project there, life was sailing.

One day, sitting in my flat with Roy, I received a call from Kanika.

"Hey, wassup?" Kanika said.

"Nothing. Just sitting in my room, with Roy."

"Oh, how's he? And ask him why has he completely disappeared for the last few days?"

"Yeah, I know he has. Now he just sits in his room and does something on the laptop all day long," I said, looking at him.

"Yeah, tell him to get excited. I am coming to your flat."

"Oh, in that case, shouldn't I be the one getting excited?"

"No, no. I'm getting Maansi along too. So tell him to shave his face and all," she said.

"Okay. I will tell him," I said and hung up.

Roy didn't only shave his face, he also took a shower and finally ironed his clothes after many weeks. By the time Kanika and Maansi walked in, Roy had already undergone a mini makeover since morning.

Roy and Maansi had been talking on and off. But as Kanika had expected, there were no real sparks. She was right. Roy was almost there, but he didn't make the cut for her.

"Hey guys," Kanika said, walking into the flat.

After her, Maansi walked in, radiating all the goodness in the world. She had an innocent smile on her face. I shook her hand and I felt as if I hadn't ever had a warmer hand shake. But then, I recalled what Roy had told me after his date with her – she is consistently nice. You can tell nothing from the way she looks at you. She is just too nice for this world. And you cannot derive anything from what you see.

They took their seats. And so did Roy. I would have expected Roy to be a little nervous. From what I had heard of his first date, it seemed he had been pretty nervous then too. But somehow, that day, he seemed to radiate a confidence which was very uncanny of him. And I could see that it was not fake at all. It was genuine. He was living it.

"So Roy, where have you been?" Kanika asked him, straight away.

"Well, I've been working on something. It's keeping me rather occupied."

"What are you working on? College projects?" Kanika asked.

"Naah. I want to keep it to myself. Allow me this little secret."

"C'mon Roy. Please tell us!" Kanika said. Roy took a lot of convincing, but she somehow managed to get it out of him.

"I am working on my first novel," he announced.

"Oh my God!" "Are you serious?" "What the fuck?" were the reactions of Kanika, Maansi and me, respectively.

"Yeah, I had always wanted to write one. And in Zeeshan's engagement, when I saw Arshi's reaction on reading what I had written, I realized it is time. It's now or never. So yeah, I've started."

After he told us, it all made sense – his running away from the party and being busy on his laptop all day long. Now we knew!

"You have completely lost your mind," I said, but everyone ignored me.

"So what is the novel about?" Maansi asked.

"Well, it's about romance. Basically, a love story," Roy said, suddenly sounding like the most sensible guy around.

A 'wow' escaped Maansi's mouth. But for the first time, there was a contemplative brief silence in the room, understanding what Roy had just said.

Kanika was the first one to break the silence. "Whose story is it? I mean, is it fictional?"

"It's a story of a guy very similar to me."

We were now beginning to accept the fact. Roy had successfully managed to drive the fact home that he was writing a book.

"Okay. But Roy, what do you know about romance? I mean, who is the love interest of the guy who is similar to you?" Kanika asked him. Roy had her attention completely.

Kanika exchanged a little glance with Maansi, who got a little uncomfortable.

There was only one anticipation hanging in the room, that was – whether Roy writing a book about Maansi or not. Roy seemed uncomfortable answering that question. And he took a while before he would answer.

"Well, actually, the female protagonist is inspired by you, Kanika," Roy said.

"What!" "Kanika!" "*Kya!*"

"Yeah," Roy continued. "Actually, you are the only girl I've got to know for a long time now. So it made sense to create a character inspired by you."

"Oh my God," Kanika said, and got up from the sofa on which she was sitting. She took a few steps forward and hugged Roy. He deserved it. Being dedicated a whole book, this was seriously big shit.

"So how does it feel?" finally Maansi spoke, after the long silence.

"To be honest, there is no better feeling in the world. It is such a meditative trance. I just love the feeling," Roy said.

"Great. I'm sure it feels awesome," Maansi said.

"Yeah. And I can already see a change in myself. I mean, now that I'm much busier than I used to be, I feel I have become more confident. My self-worth has increased. I feel better about myself."

We all nodded in unison.

At the same moment, Roy and I sneaked a glance at Maansi, to check how she received the news that Roy was writing a book based on Kanika.

And then, both of us saw it. It couldn't have been missed. Maansi finally gave him that look of genuine admiration that he had been waiting for. The fact that he was writing a book had made him come across as a much more sensible person.

Roy must have high-fived himself inside his head. It was game on.

I looked at Kanika. She was still giggling on the prospect of having a book written on her. But she didn't know what I knew. That Roy had always liked her. And it was more than obvious that the character would be based on her.

But I had nothing to worry about. Roy was a sensible fellow. And had definitely moved on, now that Maansi was in the picture.

So that was the turning point of the relationship between Maansi and him. The book had done the trick for him in crossing the threshold and becoming a likeable guy for Maansi. The next thing they knew – they were spending hours discussing the book every day. She was reading every chapter as he wrote. His initial apprehension that Maansi might not like the fact that the female protagonist was Kanika also vanished soon after.

And slowly and gradually, it was for everyone to see that romance was brewing in the air. The ultra-sophisticated girl had fallen for the guy next door. Normally, Roy was in love with every girl by default. But this time, he seemed to have genuinely fallen for her. They seemed good together. Nice and content.

But then again, there was another threshold to be crossed. Roy was supposed to tell her how he felt for her.

"It has to be something grand," I advised him one evening, when we were discussing how he was going to confess his love for Maansi.

"Are you crazy? I was thinking more like just casually telling her that I love her, without making a big deal out of it."

"See Roy, you get only one shot at telling her how you feel about her. You cannot afford to mess it up."

"I'm not going to mess it up. I know what I am doing," Roy said matter-of-factly.

"C'mon. You have to confess it in a way that she has just no other option than saying yes. In a kind of way that I said it."

"How did you say it?"

"Well, I had prepared for hours for my confession," I said, as I dazed back to the memory of that fateful day. "I just thought that if I am able to revive the memories of all the wonderful times we had had together, it should be enough to overwhelm her emotionally. So I collected all the SMSs I had sent her. And wrote them down on some chits of paper and put them on the wall of my room."

"Oh God. That's the most gay thing I've ever heard," Roy said.

"It was awesome. Even though it didn't really go the way I had hoped."

"But I don't want to make it such a big deal. I just want to tell her and get it done with."

"But Roy! You get only one chance of doing this! Don't mess it up!" I persisted.

Roy looked at me, but took out the mobile from his pocket and dialled Maansi's number. The next thing I knew, he was on phone with her.

"Hi Maansi. How are you?" Roy said and turned the phone on speaker.

"I'm good. Calling for some special reason? I mean – I'm kind of in the middle of something..." Maansi said.

"It'll take just a minute. There was something I wanted to tell you."

"Sure. You're done with the thirteenth chapter?" she asked.

"No. It's not about the book."

"Then?"

"I love you, Maansi," Roy said, just like that, as if he was saying I just had tea. In a flat tone, with no background, no build up, no context whatsoever. As if, there was not a single bit of doubt in his mind that she loved him as well.

But Maansi was silent on hearing it, as Roy and I waited in anticipation. And then, she laughed. As she kept laughing without saying anything, our heartbeats soared. We were getting impatient.

"Say something," Roy said, interjecting her laugh.

"What do you want me to say, Roy?"

"Tell me that you love me too."

"Roy?" Maansi's tone changed. Suddenly, her laughter vanished. Her voice carried all the emotion that Roy's missed.

"Yes."

"I love you too."

There. She said it as well. They were officially two people very much in love. Roy's arms went up in relief and he stepped forward and hugged me, even though I was not the person he wanted to hug at that moment.

"So?" I said, looking at him.

"So?"

"Go see her, you idiot!"

Roy left the house immediately to see Maansi. I felt happy for them. They were an awkward couple but they seemed just so happy together that you often didn't realize it.

I called up Kanika, to break the news to her. And she was ecstatic.

"Great. So where is Roy now?"

"He has gone to meet her. They must be celebrating. Dinner or something I guess."

"Hmm," Kanika said. When Kanika said 'hmm', it normally meant some bad news for me. I had a good feeling I knew which bad news was about to hit me.

"It's been so long since we went out for dinner," Kanika said softly.

"Yeah. We can go today?" I said. I knew I had to do instant damage control and I did.

"You're lucky you said that, because otherwise, you would have had it," she said, trying to sound all scary. I just found it immensely cute.

"I'm not lucky. I'm just talented," I said.

Kanika and I had seriously not been out for pretty long. So the dinner was going to be a nice change. I was looking forward to see Kanika dress up, for the first time after Zeeshan's engagement.

Honestly, I needed that. You need to go out with your girl sometimes. Dress up for her. Buy her flowers. Open the door for her. Pull the chair for her. Smell her exquisite perfume. Make her feel attractive. Create and feel the warmth in the air.

That was the thing I loved the most about her. She made me desire these little joys. She made me want to make her feel attractive. And that in itself made me feel good about myself.

The dinner was a nice and pleasant one. We came back to my flat. Kanika accompanied me to my room. And we spent the night engulfed in each other's warmth. Contended.

7

The Spirit of Leaving

Two more months passed.

Roy and Maansi became a steady couple. They developed their own joys, the things both of them could do together, in spite of being so different from each other. Just over a period of two months, Roy had changed a lot as a person. On one side, he was actually writing a book, which sky-rocketed his appeal to women. On the other side, he had a rather enviable girlfriend who kept him very busy.

Our flat had transformed from being an all-guys place to a couple hangout. It was good to have a friend couple. Now that Kanika and I were not organizing any events, it was good to have a couple around. It gave us more things to talk about. And it also made time fly by faster.

One morning, it struck me that Roy was supposed to complete an assignment the previous night. So I walked into his room.

"Roy, did you finish the assignment?" I asked. But when I saw his face, I saw the saddest expression I had ever seen on his face. I knew the reason – Maansi was going away for seven days. I was planning to pull his leg about being such a girl about it, but he seemed as if he had just been hit by a tsunami.

So, I did what any good friend must do in such a situation.

I decided to pull his leg even more.

"Oh, Ms Roy, seems like I walked in on your period," I chuckled. But Roy wasn't very receptive to the humour.

"What do you want, Samar?"

"Where is Maansi going that it is killing you so bad?"

"Well, it's some Sri Guru camp in Bangalore. Her family is a staunch believer in him. So she has to attend this camp," he said.

"You mean to say her father is making her attend it?"

"No, no. She is herself a believer. She wants to attend this. And there are no cell phones allowed for one week."

"Oh okay," I said, ending the discussion on her. "Did you do that assignment?"

He did not. Roy used that week to get drenched in the writing process. All day long, he just wrote and wrote. He had no phone calls or naughty thoughts to distract him. I liked what this girl was doing to him.

Kanika and I looked at him, being locked up in his room all day, coming out only for coffee and meals. We felt happy for him.

Maansi's phone finally came back on a week later. Roy had been calling her nonstop, since morning. And when his phone finally got through, he took a sigh of relief.

But Maansi rejected his call. It was a knife through Roy's heart.

What? Roy typed and sent to her.

Roy, I need to talk to you. But not right now. Will call you in the night.

Roy read her reply. And it sent chills through his spine. Maansi needed to *talk*. It didn't sound too good. Roy had somehow made it through the week. But this day was going to be a tough one now. I felt a little angry at Maansi. A little longer text message, telling what all this was about wouldn't have hurt her. She must have expected Roy to be perturbed on reading the text message. And she wasn't dumb enough to have missed such an obvious thing.

Maansi finally called at eleven in the night. And the moment her name flashed on his phone, Roy stood up and left for his room. And I went to my room and started watching some sitcom. When I was done with two episodes, my thoughts went back to Roy. I checked his door. It was still locked. He must still be on the phone, I concluded.

Two episodes later, I went back to check in his room. His door was shut but not locked. I checked to hear any sounds. There were none. I presumed he had hung up. So I decided to walk in.

I walked in and the sight that awaited me, shook me. Roy was lying on his bed, with his eyes closed. And there were tears on his cheeks. I had never seen any of my guy friends cry.

It was more than obvious that Maansi had just broken up with him. I was curious for the reason but I had little doubt that knowing it would make me less angry at her.

On seeing me, Roy's expression didn't change. The tears in his eyes spoke volumes, even though the rest of his face was rather blank.

A 'why' escaped my lips.

"Her guruji in Bangalore has told her not to get into this relationship. It can harm her family and me. And she never does anything against her guruji's wish," he said.

"Maansi doesn't come across as someone who would follow a guruji."

"But I know she does follow everything this Guruji says. He is the head of that Spirit of Living thing. He is quite renowned."

"Okay. So is it over?" I asked.

"Yeah. Seems so. I mean Maansi is not the kind of girl who breaks up several times to patch up again. She is quite strong headed."

I looked at Roy. It was as if he was paying back for receiving so much joy for the last two months. There is not much a guy can say to a guy in such a case. Except maybe one thing that can be said.

"Beer?" I asked.

"No, Samar. I'm not in the mood. I need some time alone."

"Okay," I said and left the room. And called up Kanika to fill her in on what happened.

"Was he actually crying?" Kanika asked, a little surprised, a little sad.

"Yeah. With genuine tears."

"Hmm. Let's leave him alone today. We'll talk to him tomorrow."

"Are you going to talk to Maansi?" I asked.

"Naah. I don't think she will be in the mood either."

"Okay," I said and hung up.

The next morning was a sombre one. Roy was quiet, I was quiet. Conversation was impossible because if we talked, it would have been impossible to talk about anything other than the break up. And the break up was a topic rather out of bounds.

We reached college, without exchanging a single word since morning. We sat silently through the lectures. There was only one way our silences were going to break – Kanika.

During the lunch break, we met Kanika at the canteen. She approached our table and looked at me. That look only meant one thing. She wanted to talk to Roy alone. This was a first. But then, it was also necessary. So I went for a solitary walk away from them.

As Kanika and Roy talked, I realized how empty my college life was without them both. In the process of having built cement strong bonds with them, I had also ended up alienating myself with everybody in college. I wasn't complaining. They were the ideal companions to have for your college life. If anything, I was only lucky.

I walked back into the canteen a little while later. Kanika and Roy were not there anymore.

Where are you? I messaged Kanika.

She didn't reply for pretty long. So I decided to walk back to my flat. It was a little weird walking back alone after classes. I couldn't recall the last time Roy was not with me on this walk back.

When I reached my flat, I realized Kanika and Roy were there, in Roy's room. I peeped in through the little door opening. Roy was looking kind of messed up. He was again, on the brink of tears. Finally, he was opening his heart in front of someone. I was not surprised at all, that that someone was Kanika. She was making him talk, and cleanse all his negative feelings in the process.

I decided not to interrupt in the session. And decided to walk back to my room as nondescriptly as I had entered.

I had never imagined a girl could do this to Roy. In fact, I had never imagined a girl could do anything of this sort to any guy. Thank God Kanika was there to take care of him. She was a sensible girl; the kind of person you need to get out of such a situation. And thinking of her at Roy's elbow, I somehow felt good about the fact that she was my girl. I had made a good choice. Or had been plain lucky.

8
A thousand deaths
every minute

I had expected Roy to improve over time. I mean, I was expecting him to at least start smiling in a week's time. And to forget all about Maansi in a month. But it didn't happen.

It had been a month and I still hadn't seen him smile. He was taking it really badly, much worse than I could have ever imagined. We had our fifth semester final exams going on. And even though Roy had never been a star in the exams, his concentration had visibly waivered. There is this thing about exams and me – I somehow brave through most of them. But when it comes to *the* last exam, I tend to succumb to my urge of goofing around.

So the evening before the final exam, instead of giving final touches to my preparations, I felt like breaking out of my flat, and take a walk or go to meet a friend or something. And whenever I get such a feeling, only one name comes to my mind – Zeeshan.

I hadn't seen much of him ever since he had gotten engaged. His priorities in life had changed. And knowing Arshi, I knew he must be putting in a lot of effort in staying her fiancé.

Zeeshan and I had met because I had always wanted to play the guitar and the first time I had seen him, he was carrying one. One thing led to another and half an hour later, I was sitting in his living room, holding the guitar. At that time, his house was broken shit. But then, Kanika and I had helped him make the place liveable when we had become friends. But ever since Arshi had come in his life, the place had really begun to sparkle.

So this day, again, I picked my guitar and started walking towards Zeeshan's house.

When I entered, Zeeshan was on the phone. He was shouting at somebody.

"No, I cannot come to meet your *Baja.*"

"No, I do not have any important work but I am just fed up meeting your two thousand relatives," Zeeshan said and disconnected the call, furiously.

Just as he hung up the phone, he noticed me standing in the room. "Dude, whatever you do, don't get married."

"But Arshi is a nice girl. I mean – look at you. You used to be neglected wreck when you met her. And today, you generate respect in whoever comes inside your house."

"But what if I don't *want* that respect? What if I *want* to live the way I used to? What if I liked living in a mess, because it meant I didn't spend one hour everyday making sure this place is clean?"

Zeeshan had a point. The first time I had met him, his lack of desire for cleanliness had very much been apparent.

"Relax, Zeeshan. Arshi is a nice girl," I maintained.

"I have no doubt that she is. But I kind of need a break now. I need to get away from her or something."

"What do you mean?"

"I'm taking the train to Goa tomorrow evening. A few days there will clear my mind," he said.

"Oh no, you are doing no such thing."

"I've already booked a ticket. In fact, you know what? You should also come along."

Zeeshan had once been deeply into smoking cigarettes and weed. But over the months, he had managed to wean himself away from everything. But the way he was talking about Goa that day, it was more than obvious that he was going back to all that, at least temporarily, while he would be there.

"Oh no, thank you. I'm working on a project after my final exam tomorrow."

"Projects and exams will come and go, brother. But Goa will never return. Fuck everything and come with me."

"I'm a third year student, Zeeshan. Next year, all the companies will be swarming across to throw jobs at me. I need this project in this vacation."

I threw a thousand logics at him to convince him and myself that I couldn't afford this trip. And we got back to doing what we enjoyed doing the most together. We played our guitars a little.

I walked back to my flat and opened my books. I heard some sound from Roy's room and decided to see what was happening. Roy was on the phone, presumably with Kanika. They had come really close now. Kanika was probably spending more time on phone with him than me. The break up, Roy's book, college, life... they had a lot of things to talk about.

Once again, I decided not to disturb him and went to sleep.

When we were in school, the guy who left the examination hall before everybody else was assumed to know everything. In college, the guy who left before everybody else was supposed to know nothing. Roy was that guy in the final exam. I didn't expect him to care too much about this one. He was just in a hurry to declare that his exams were now over.

But I was more of a fighter. No matter how little I knew in

the exam, I couldn't help trying till the last minute. That day was no different.

By the time my exam ended, I was dead tired. Normally, end of exams define a spurt of energy. But by the fifth semester, one tends to have mellowed down. Kanika and Roy, both were nowhere in sight. And I had no plans of indulging in post-exam discussions like 'how did it go?' or 'what was the answer to this question?'

Strangely, end of exams gave me a strong urge to go back to my flat and go to sleep. So I walked back to my flat, without calling or messaging anyone. I just thought I would reach my bed and die. I reached my flat and realized that the door was open. That meant Roy was home. I assumed he must have been waiting for the exams to get over to get back to his novel. I almost envied his focus. He had finally found two important things he had really needed. It was like every time he had a minute free, he didn't have to think what to do with it.

Also, he had finally made a good friend apart from me – Kanika. They seemed happy when they were together, which was another positive. These girls should always have something to do. Because if they don't, they start sulking and make your life hell.

I opened Roy's room's door and looked in.

And what I saw decided the course of the rest of my life.

Roy and Kanika kissing each other.

I couldn't believe what I was seeing. Kanika was lying on Roy's bed and Roy was lying over her. And his lips were frantically kissing hers. Kanika's eyes were closed in ecstasy. They didn't even realize I was standing there.

My vision blurred. I felt like I was collapsing. I thought I was going to reduce to a bundle of sand then and there, at my own doorstep. Maybe my eyes were playing tricks with me. This could not be. This simply could not be. But it really was her. There was no mistaking. She was lying on the bed with her eyes closed, as he kissed her frantically.

It was something I would not even want my worst enemies to go through. If I had a weak heart, it was worthy of a heart attack. I could so clearly hear it in my chest. My thighs were shaking. This couldn't have been happening.

Kanika. No. No. No.

My eyes blacked out. My brain froze. The blood in my veins stopped flowing. Everything around me was rotating. I could not decipher what I was seeing. And I could not make sense of any sounds coming from around me.

This can't be happening. But it *was* happening. It was right in front of my eyes. They were so engrossed in kissing that they didn't even realize I was standing there. Roy. One guy I had always believed will never fuck me in the ass. Why couldn't I see it earlier? I had always believed him to be the guy who talked desperate but was always the sweet one. But from now on, every time I would look at him, I would want to break his teeth.

Why did he have to do this? Was a girl really that important? Couldn't he find some other girl in the whole wide world? Kanika? *My Kanika?* And Kanika? How could she? How could she find it in herself to kiss someone else? That too – my best friend? It looked like a cruel joke to me.

I turned around and slammed the door behind me. Roy must have finally noticed me by the sound of the door being closed. I heard a sound come from inside "*Samar?*" But I didn't react. I kept walking out. I turned around and stumbled on my way out but I recovered. I crossed the road. I waited across the road to see if Roy would come outside to check on me.

I kept waiting for a good five minutes but neither of them came out. I lost my senses. First they decide to betray me like that, and then they don't even have the decency to even try to apologize to me? Or at least explain what happened? Did our relationship have so less significance in their lives? Roy? Kanika?

Did I mean so less to both of them? What did I do to deserve this? This was insane. I was going mad.

I looked at the road and the sun seemed way too bright. It was an effort to keep my eyes open. I didn't know where to go, now that my house was the last place I wanted to be in.

Amongst the worst of things my brain had ever been able to conjure, this was worse. Kanika kissing Roy. Trust me, I cannot mean it more, when I say – I would have truly loved to die before seeing what I had. The traffic on the road seemed dangerous for a second. And then it almost seemed tempting. It felt inviting to me. My head was clouded with suicidal thoughts. I felt like succumbing to the temptation. Just one moment of pain and then redemption, forever. It would definitely be better than this lifelong humiliation, where I would have to die a thousand deaths every minute. I couldn't think of a good reason for not succumbing.

My eyes were bloodshot. I had no recollection of when I had torn my shirt. I was almost murderous at that moment. And then another thought came to my mind. It was they who were screwing around. It is them who should be messed up, not me. In fact, what I should do is go back to that room and give them a piece of my mind. A punch or two would help. I suddenly felt a very strong urge to go and punch Roy in the face. That should ease the pain a lot.

But somehow, I could not bring myself to see their faces again. I wanted to run away. Just silently disappear. Just take a random train and disappear at a place where even I wouldn't find myself.

I hailed an auto and sat in it. I just wanted to run away from this place and spend some time where I would not have to see any familiar faces. Maybe some street where I can just walk, without looking like a lunatic.

"Where do you want to go?" the auto driver asked.

"Connaught Place," I heard myself say. A circular road with

a bunch of people aimlessly walking seemed like a good idea.

I thought of Kanika and the one year of knowing her, passed through my eyes. Our first meeting, our first conversation, our first touch, our first kiss. I pictured it all in front of my eyes. And the more I thought of it, the worse I felt. Somebody kill me, I was thinking.

Just then, I saw a couple passing across me. I looked at them and every cell in my body wanted to go up to the guy and tell him to run. I wanted to tell him to run, before the girl messed up his life and left him devastated, just as I was.

It was a feeling which only very few people must have experienced. It was worse than the death of someone close. Death is definitive. And there is a reason. This seemed to have no reason.

It was a pure slap on the face. A bullet in the back.

Roy. All the great times we had had. All the dreams and aspirations we had shared. We had talked about going on a world tour on our fortieth birthdays. And he had cut short the friendship in the most brutal fashion. It was beyond my imagination or understanding.

I kept my head in my lap and resolved I would not cry. I maintained a stoic face and fought the tears in my eyes. Somehow, in spite of the heavy resistance, a tiny drop made its way out, which I brushed away angrily. I saw myself in the rear view mirror of the auto. I hadn't looked more hateful to myself, ever before.

No.

The next time I got a grasp of where I was, I had reached Connaught Place. I looked all around. Everyone was carrying out their businesses as if nothing new had happened today. They will do the same thing they did yesterday. Some of them were hoping to earn more money today. But no one of them had been slapped in the face the way I had been.

For them, today was a photocopy of yesterday.

But for me, this was the defining hour. I would never be able to look back at my life and not think of this hour. I just wanted to run away.

I heard a group of young girls laugh loudly and I turned around. I was curious if they knew my secret. I wondered if they were saying within their group 'this guy's girlfriend kissed his roommate' as they laughed. But they weren't. They were laughing on an inside joke.

Just then my phone started to vibrate in my pocket. I wondered if I wanted it to be Kanika or not. I just couldn't decide.

I took out the phone from my pocket. It was Zeeshan.

"Hi Zeeshan," I said, receiving the call.

"Samar. Are you coming or not?" he asked.

"Coming where?"

"Goa, you idiot. I told you yesterday evening," he said.

"I don't know, Zeeshan," I said.

"But I know. You are coming with me."

"I don't feel like," I said in a very feeble voice. I didn't have the energy to argue.

"I know you do feel like and I know you really want to come too. Meet me at the railway station as soon as you can," Zeeshan said and hung up.

I was dazed, not very clear about what was happening around me. Like a zombie, I entered the Metro and reached New Delhi Railway Station. It's only ten minutes from Connaught Place which didn't really allow my crowded brain to think much.

I climbed the train to Goa, found a corner to sit and closed my eyes. I hadn't realized how tired I had got by then. It was still the same day. I had woken up early to study for the last exam of the semester. I had studied till 1:45 in the afternoon and had then taken the exam.

And then I had seen the image which will be permanently

printed in front of my eyes, forever.

I sat next to the door, listening to all the conversations happening around me. In the box next to mine, two guys were talking.

"So how was your date with her?" one of them asked the other.

"It was okay," the other guy replied.

"Oh. So you didn't get to kiss her?"

"Yeah. We kissed. But it was okay."

"You kissed her! That's great, man. How was it?" the first guy asked.

"It wasn't great. She didn't let me do anything else."

"But still! You kissed her! I didn't know you were so deeply in love!"

"Just because I kissed her doesn't mean I am in love with her," the second guy said.

"So you kissed her just like that?"

"Yeah… A kiss means nothing, man. "

"So you won't even marry her?" the first guy asked. And second guy started laughing loudly, as if this was the funniest thing he had ever heard.

I didn't know what to think. Thoughts flooded my mind but nothing seemed to settle. Was Kanika's kiss with Roy as irrelevant as this guy's kiss with his girl? Or were they *my* kisses with Kanika that were irrelevant to her?

Suddenly I couldn't take it anymore. Sitting alone, brooding over what had happened was only making the matter worse. I felt like going to the toilet but getting up was a huge task because of the tiredness. I somehow mustered the energy anyway. With the help of the washbasin, I managed to pull myself up. I came back to where I had been sitting and looked out of the train. And then began my battle with unshed tears. *I would not cry.*

9

Life is a Beach

M y eyes opened at five in the morning. I looked all around to see where I was.

For a second, I got scared. When I opened my eyes, the first thing I saw was the bottom view of a dingy wash basin. A dirty smell hit my nostrils. I was sitting quite close to the toilet.

And then the same scene flash crossed my eyes. The visual of Kanika kissing Roy. The girl who was my First Love.

I got up from there and walked away from the toilet to escape the stink. I went and stood in the middle of the bogey. Everybody was asleep. I had no luggage. My only belongings were my wallet and my phone in my pocket. I tried to figure out what to do next.

I called up Zeeshan. He didn't pick the call, as expected. You can expect him to not go to sleep till the wee hours of the morning but waking up at 5 is something he can never achieve.

So in the dead of the night, I went to the door of the bogey, hung my legs outside and sat. I liked the wind on my face. I tried to think about something pleasant, so that I wouldn't think of her. It was futile. All I could think of was what I had seen earlier that day. As I sat there, trying to fight back the storm of emotions, images from the relationship I had had with Kanika flashed through my mind. We had had good times, we had had bad ones too. But we had been in it together.

What we had faced in one and half year was a lot more than what a lot of people face in a lifetime. And we had been able to do it only because we knew we had each other by our sides, no matter what.

That wasn't true anymore.

With that kiss, everything had shattered. There was nothing left between us. We were over. The thought was too painful for me to even think of.

An hour later, people began to wake up. I indulged in watching their faces and trying to understand what they were going to do in Goa. Goa always attracted a nice mix of people. And watching them and guessing what was going on in their minds was an ideal way to ignore what was going on in *my* mind. I needed the distraction.

At 7, I tried Zeeshan's number once again.

"Hello," he said, in a very sleepy voice. I tried to listen hard to make out if he was in the train. The last thing I wanted was that I had climbed the train but he had changed his plans. The last thing I wanted was to be alone in a foreign city. Or maybe, when I thought of it I felt, it wouldn't be all that bad.

But it was hard to make out from his background sounds when there was so much noise around me. And I realized it would be impossible to explain to him everything when he is this sleepy. So I disconnected the call.

Zeeshan called me back fifteen minutes later.

"Hi Samar," Zeeshan said.

"Hey. Did you finally leave for Goa?" I asked.

"How does it matter to you? You ditched me, bastard!" Zeeshan said.

"Just answer the question. Did you leave for Goa or not?" I asked.

"I am on the train right now, alone, to myself. And it feels blissful already!"

"Which bogey are you in?"

"Why? Are you on the train too?" he asked.

"Yes. I am in S2. Come here. I am sitting at the rear door," I said and hung up. And I got back to looking out of the train door, with my feet hanging outside. I saw the landscape pass under my feet. And when the train crossed a bridge, I looked at the water below. Ugly thoughts started crossing my mind seeing the water below. I was only one small push away from putting an end to all my miseries. One second of courage could end everything.

Just then, Zeeshan touched my shoulder from the back and I stood up. We were not the hugging types but both of us were smiling. Definitely my first smile since *that* moment.

"I'm glad you came, man. But how? I thought you ditched me," Zeeshan said.

"It was a last minute thing. I thought I would sit here for a while before calling you and didn't realize when I fell asleep," I said.

"Okay. You must be tired sleeping here. Come, let's go to my seat," Zeeshan said.

I started walking.

"But where is your bag?"

"I didn't get any," I said and smiled.

"And money?"

"Just enough to buy us breakfast," I said. Zeeshan grinned.

And we started walking towards his bogey, inside the train.

The rest of the journey was fractionally better. With Zeeshan by my side, I at least had some distraction. And I didn't care where I was, as long as I was nowhere near my flat.

I had never gone on a tour that was so completely unplanned. And it felt odd. Add to that, the only clothes I had were the ones on my body and the only money I owned was whatever there was in my wallet.

As scary as it felt for a minute, it felt equally thrilling too.

~

Sitting in the train, I kept undergoing mood swings. One moment I was alright. Another I was furious. And at moments, sitting in front of Zeeshan, looking out of the window, for no particular reason, I got really, really furious.

At one such moment, my phone started vibrating. I took it out of my pocket and Roy's name flashed on the screen. On some other moment, I might have contemplated receiving the call. But at this moment, seeing his name gave me a strong urge to throw my phone out of the window.

But I resisted it. Even if I wanted to not keep my phone, it could have had better use than being thrown out, especially now that I didn't have much money in my pocket.

So I settled for switching it off and keeping it back in my pocket. And I realized I had no idea who else was sitting in our box in the train, apart from Zeeshan and me.

For a very brief second, I imagined myself being swarmed by a bunch of good looking girls. But when I looked around, I was expectedly let down. There were no girls around.

I realized that in the process of all the turmoil, I had also just turned single. I wouldn't have to strangle the urge to talk to a good looking girl on the road. And considering the fact that I was going to a place with the hottest girls in the country, I should have felt good about it.

And yet, I didn't. Somehow, then, I wanted to feel that strangulation of not being able to check out any girl. I wanted to feel the stability of being in love with her.

Train journeys can be very boring. The uncle-*ji* sitting beside me didn't make matters any easier. Firstly, he was carrying an extremely repulsive smell of spices. It was quite a task sitting within a few inches from him. And then, the fact that he was distinctly ugly didn't make him any bearable. It seemed as if he really needed a bath, even though he must have definitely had a shower the same morning. Also, my impatience and the long journey to Goa, made it all the more unpleasant.

"So where are you guys from?" the middle aged man said, rubbing his pot belly. As if his presence wasn't annoying enough, he wanted to talk now.

"Delhi," I replied, in as short a way as I could.

"Holiday plans in Goa?"

"Yeah." He was beginning to get on my nerve.

"What is your name?" he asked, pestering to continue the conversation.

"Samar."

"Zeeshan."

"What kind of party are you looking for?" he asked us.

I was in no mood of replying to that. I suddenly wanted silence. I contemplated going to the washroom, just to escape this conversation.

"Anything will do, actually," Zeeshan replied. "Wherever we can have some fun and meet some new people."

"Actually, I know one such party which I'm sure you two will love," the man said.

Suddenly, he captured my interest. I hadn't given him much chance from his demeanour. But still, I wanted to hear what he had to say.

"What are you talking about?" Zeeshan said.

"This is my phone number. If you want to go to a wild party where very few people go, give me a call."

Zeeshan took his number and shook his hand.

"What is your name, sir?" Zeeshan asked.

"Thimappa Vajramatti."

"What?"

"Thimappa Vajramatti."

"What?"

"Thi-ma-ppa Vaj-ra-matti."

"Ok," both of us said, giving up on trying to make out.

The train reached Goa and we got off it. We faked a final smile and said good bye to the Thimpa man in the train. Just as we made our way out of the station, three gorgeous girls crossed us in very short clothes. Zeeshan and I looked at each other and it finally hit us big time.

We were in Goa!

Goa. One answer to everything wrong that can happen. It was supposed to make me leave behind all the negativity. Most importantly, it was supposed to help me get rid of that visual, of seeing Kanika and Roy in a lip locked state.

Finally, I felt a little better after the extreme feeling in the pit of my stomach for so many hours. We hired a cab and headed to the Calangute beach, to look for a hotel.

"So what kind of a hotel are we moving into?" I asked Zeeshan.

"Obviously, the best one in Goa."

"You are forgetting I am not carrying enough money with me."

"Fuck you, man. Why couldn't you just carry an ATM card?" Zeeshan said.

"We will argue about this later. For now, we are moving into a very cheap hotel on the beach."

"Whatever," Zeeshan said, conceding.

We checked into a pretty cheap hotel on the beach which had an adjoining shack. If you have never been to Goa, then shacks are Goan style restaurants on the beach which have armchairs where people relax and drink. Those who didn't drink prefer to eat.

The room was small and dirty. But it was cheap enough. Zeeshan was sulking visibly about the room. He wanted to make it as clear as possible that he didn't like this. That too when his own place was several times worse than this only a little time ago.

I ignored him as my thoughts went back to *her*. I looked

around the room. I saw the dressing table. I saw the beach outside the window. I saw a pretty girl in an orange top.

Unfortunately, absolutely everything took my thoughts back to her. The dressing table reminded me of her combing her hair. The beach reminded me of the time we had spent on the beach the previous year. The girl in the orange top reminded me of her orange top.

I realized that I needed some time before my thoughts would stabilize. Until then, I was basically screwed.

"So, what's the plan?" I asked.

"I need to catch some sleep first," Zeeshan said.

"No. We're not going to sit in the hotel at all," I said. I need time outdoors. I needed to see some pleasant sights to feel a little better.

Zeeshan was taken aback by my firmness. But as usual, he behaved like a good friend and agreed to go out.

"So where do we start?" Zeeshan asked.

Once we were out, the same thing struck both of us. Neither of us had any clue what people did in Goa in the day. We looked around and tried to make out what people were doing.

"Do you want to soak up the sun? Maybe get a tan?" Zeeshan asked.

"Do I look like someone who needs a tan?" I said, pointing towards my already dusky skin.

"Then what do you want to do?"

Just then, a bunch of white girls passed us, riding two small scooters.

"Are you thinking what I'm thinking?" Zeeshan asked.

"Yeah. Why not?" I said. And just then it struck me. I was single and had every right to get excited on seeing those girls. But wasn't Zeeshan engaged to my friend? Why was he getting excited on seeing the girls?

"So where do we get these? I want the same one that hottie has," Zeeshan said.

"Zeeshan, are you planning to hit on them?"

"Yeah. Actually I am. But don't worry. If you like any of them, I'll keep away from here."

"And what about your girl?" I asked.

"It's okay. It's my bachelor's party. I'm allowed to do that."

"I can't let you do this."

"Look, Samar," Zeeshan said, firmly, "I have decided to spend the rest of my life with Arshi once we get married. It takes guts to make such a commitment. But until I'm married, I'll kiss whoever I want to."

I looked at him. The mention of the word *kiss* inevitably took my thoughts back to Kanika. And then I realized, that maybe this is how the world works. And maybe I shouldn't intervene. If this is what he wanted to do, I should accept it and mind my own fucking business.

So we hired a motorcycle each.

"Let's go then," I said.

"Yeah. Let the party begin."

"Yeah! And I didn't realize that it's your bachelor's party," I said, as both of us turned our bikes to full throttle.

We looked around the sights of Goa. A broken old fort, a lesser known beach, an ancient church and those kinds of things. They weren't particularly interesting, but they kept us occupied. And we got to see pretty faces. As the sights ended, it was already pretty dark. But more importantly, the party hours had begun!

We came back to Calangute Beach and parked our bikes outside our hotel. We washed our faces in the washroom and headed out to party, Goa style.

We headed out to the beach and started looking for the loudest party. We started walking from our hotel and went all the way up to the other end of the beach to look for the best party. And then we walked back to the one which was a clear winner. Funnily, it wasn't really the best party with the best music. It just seemed to have the hottest women and Zeeshan was completely on the prowl now. We took a table and ordered two beers each. Before the third song ended, the beer was in our tummy. And we were on the dance floor. Zeeshan started dancing. He was terrible. I tried to keep up with his terribleness. I discovered I was a natural at keeping up with his terribleness.

Once Zeeshan was drunk enough, he decided it was time to approach a girl. He spotted his target and he walked up to her, as I looked on from some distance.

"Hey, do I know you? You look like someone I know," Zeeshan said.

"Is it? Who?"

"You so look like my next girlfriend," I heard Zeeshan say.

The girl was terribly put off by that and she walked away. Zeeshan wasn't disheartened. He moved onto the next girl. And then the next. And then the next. With the same sad pick-up line.

One bottle of beer in his hand and a smile on his face, Zeeshan tried pretty hard, until he had tried on almost every single girl in that club. And once he was done, he came back to our table.

"Samar, there is something I want to tell you."

"Yes?" I said, gearing up for something really heavy coming my way.

"Brother, I'm really scared of getting married!"

I looked at him and he was half crying and half laughing. I didn't know how to react. But then, with as many beers down as he had, most things seem happy. So we both laughed.

"But why? You shouldn't—"

"Because I *fucking* don't want to get married!"

"Then what do you want to do?" I asked.

"I want to fool around in clubs in Goa. I want to hit on random girls in spite of knowing I don't stand a chance. I want to climb on this table and have a drinking race with you!"

"You know what..."

"What?" Zeeshan said.

"Let's do it!" I said and climbed on the table. Zeeshan followed suit and climbed the table too with his bottle of beer in his hand.

The next thing we knew, the whole club was looking at us. And we had a bottle of beer in our hands each.

And then, someone started a countdown.

3...

2...

1...

And we started drinking from our bottles, simultaneously. Within sixty seconds, my bottle was empty. I looked at Zeeshan, hoping to find him still drinking. But he wasn't there standing beside me. He wasn't there on the table. And I couldn't see him even in the club. Just then, I noticed some activity at the club door. Some bouncers were throwing Zeeshan out for climbing on the table.

Once he was thrown, the Bouncers started walking towards me. I signalled them to calm down and walked out with whatever sense I had left in me. I spotted Zeeshan, shouting fervently at the gate of the Club.

"I'm going to kill these bastards," he shouted.

"Relax, Zeeshan. Let's go to our rooms."

"Are you crazy? The party has just started."

"No, it hasn't. The party is over," I said.

"No, it's not..."

I had to literally drag Zeeshan back to our room. But then, I know what a good time for a party to get over is. It was time that we give ourselves away to the lap of drunken slumber.

"Good night, sweetheart," Zeeshan said, as I switched off the lights.

The next morning, Zeeshan woke up with a hangover. The moment I saw his morning face, I knew that we were not going anywhere that morning. I didn't mind. I left him in the bed and went for a walk to the beach. I took a seat in one of the shacks and stared at people around me. There seemed to be an interesting mix. The waiter walked up to me and asked for the order. I knew I had no money in my pocket. So I decided to walk away. A beach is one of the most serene places in the morning. So I kept walking, feeling the sand on my feet.

By the time I came back, Zeeshan still hadn't returned to his senses. He was holding his head, and coughing profusely.

"Hey, are you okay?"

"Not really," Zeeshan said. "Can you get me a pen and a paper?"

"Sure," I said, and got it from the reception.

"Here, get this from a Chemist," Zeeshan said. As unbelievable as it may sound, Zeeshan had been a doctor in an earlier life.

We spent the day in the room itself, fighting out the ugly feeling. It was around midnight that Zeeshan wanted to party again. And we went to a club and picked our bottles again. And partied the night away, once again. Nothing changed. We got majorly drunk and danced away the night.

It was the evening of the next day, that Zeeshan really sounded off.

"So, how're you liking the trip?" he asked me.

"Better than I could have asked for. What do you think?"

"Are you crazy? This is the worst trip ever! We haven't done a single unpredictable thing yet!"

"I don't like the way this conversation is shaping," I muttered.

"Shut up, Samar. Nothing has happened in this trip which we didn't expect to happen."

"So? What are you trying to say?"

"See – we've both been to Goa before. Both of us have been to the beach and had tens of beers *each*. And what we're doing now is simply not happening... I mean, I want to call that Thimpa guy from the train," Zeeshan said.

"Are you crazy? You think that guy knows a party which can be fun?"

"Honestly, I don't. But still, I want to give him a chance. You never know. At least it will be something we wouldn't have seen before."

"But what if I don't want to see what he is going to show me?" I asked.

Zeeshan shoved the thought away and called the guy anyway. I heard him talk as that Thimpa guy explained some route to him. I didn't have a good feeling about this. But Zeeshan seemed to have his heart on giving it a shot. We were walking towards the road, as Zeeshan raked every nerve of his brain trying to understand the way. And when he hung up, without asking for my agreement, Zeeshan hailed a cab and explained the way to him.

"At least tell me what is the place called?" I yelled.

"It's called WoodStock Village."

10
WoodStock Village

Most things in Goa are mostly nearby. So when the cab driver took a good twenty minutes to reach WoodStock, Zeeshan and I began to get a little irritable. We were both beginning to think it would be a waste of time. It was already late evening and we were getting nowhere.

"I'm beginning to get sober and I don't like it," I said, sitting in the back seat of that cab.

"Are we on the right path?" Zeeshan asked the driver.

"Yes."

"What do you think we will find there?" I asked Zeeshan.

"To be honest, I'm expecting a shady restaurant with some old couples sitting there," Zeeshan said.

I prayed, with whatever energy I had, that he would be wrong. I hadn't slept properly all night. I was genuinely tired. My body was crying for rest.

"Where is this place exactly?"

"There is some Arambol Village. It's in some corner there," Zeeshan replied.

We had been on the highway till now. For a tourist, most Goan roads are not all that different. But just then, the cab took a turn towards a broken road. The scenery around us changed. A sign board told me we had reached Arambol Village. The mystery of this place just kept getting higher and higher.

After a few more kilometres on the broken tread, we finally reached a place with a thatch boundary. I could see nothing except the boundary in the dark of the night, and a dim thud that indicated that loud music was being played somewhere nearby. The car entered a big gate which had WoodStock Village written over it.

Pulling us out of a trance like state, the cab driver asked us, "Are you guys from Goa?"

"No. Why?"

"Because normally only people who really know Goa very well, come to WoodStock Village. And whoever comes once, makes sure he comes here every time."

"Is it that good?" I asked.

"What exactly makes it so good?" Zeeshan added.

"In WoodStock, you kind of get everything – Food, cocktails, beer, whisky, weed…"

"We get all that almost everywhere in Goa," Zeeshan said.

"…and women," the cabbie added.

Just then, the car stopped in front of an open area. Zeeshan and I got off it and we saw the spectacular scene in front of us. We were blown away by what we saw.

In the centre, there was an open area with a stage in front of it. On the stage, I saw some foreigners with drums in their hands. They were playing some really exotic and impressive music. There was a dancer as well on the stage. In front of the stage, people were swaying to the music in the open area. Everybody seemed to be in an individual trance, as if they were in their own world. It was more than evident that most of them were stoned. My guess was that, there were some fifty people in that place but I was sure that this place deserved a lot more. It wasn't a high energy party with people jumping all over. It was a low energy, mature sort of party. People seemed way too happy to be real. In other words, they were all mindlessly *high*.

I took my eyes away from the crowd and looked around. There were small huts on two sides, which must have been lent out like in a hotel.

On the third side, there was a restaurant, where people sat on the floor and smoked tens of different things. On the fourth side, was the beach. Zeeshan and I looked at each other. Our eyes were saying the same thing. We had just reached heaven. Zeeshan mentally carried out a comparison in his mind and concluded that at least half the people in this place are females.

We high-fived like never before.

"I'm not leaving this place for at least a month," Zeeshan declared, as he dashed inside the crowd.

As Zeeshan disappeared into the crowd, even I started walking towards the crowd. And the closer I got to the area, the more excited I got. The beats of the music were entering my skin and spreading a holistic sort of euphoria in my body. It was as if I was inhaling a state of trance, which was taking over every thought in my head.

I was single. I didn't have to check my eye. I could look at whoever I wanted, unlike what it used to be when I was with *her*. Just as I was walking into the crowd, a pretty girl passed on my left. We established eye contact and I noticed a very faint smile on her face.

This was Goa. This was heaven. I kept walking towards the crowd. I noticed people grinding. I wondered how many of them knew each other before that evening. I thanked the impulse that made me come to Goa. I went to the middle of the crowd and I just looked around, to see what people were doing. There was only one common string between everybody – happiness. And wasn't that what we were all looking for?

For a moment, I thought I could do it for the rest of my life.

What is it about a stable job that everyone is after it? Why not stay here and have a higher level of happiness?

I finally spotted Zeeshan close where the artists were playing music. On seeing me, he dragged me there with him and started dancing with me. It was very unlike Zeeshan to be doing this. We normally didn't dance with each other. Suddenly Zeeshan shifted his leg and hence, he was half dancing with me and half with a foreigner girl dancing behind him. Her hair was orange-red and she seemed drunk. But what must have really got Zeeshan excited was the fact that she seemed alone.

He subtly shifted his posture and started dancing in her vicinity. Zeeshan started putting on the moves on her and then, with one clean motion, he was dancing with her.

They established eye contact and the girl continued to dance. He had managed to get her approval to dance with her.

Soon, the two of them vanished into the crowd. And I was left dancing alone. So I decided to fetch a beer and concentrate on the beer in my hand. I spotted them again about ten minutes later. They seemed pretty close now. Roy was holding the back of her head. He leaned into her and pulled her closer to himself. The next moment, their lips were locked.

The visual of the two of them kissing brought back everything I wanted to forget. My heart was beating and there might have been a drop or two of sweat on my forehead. Suddenly, I felt suffocated standing in the crowded party. I needed some fresh air.

I made my way through the crowd, into some open air. I was breathing heavily. I went and stood at some distance from the crowd, taking a deep breath. There weren't many people where I was standing. And I liked that. I had had enough alcohol and enough adventure for a day. All I needed then was some time alone.

I turned towards the beach and kept staring at the waves of the sea. It was soothing. And it served its purpose – My mind was blank. No thoughts of Kanika or Roy. Surprisingly, for all the time I stood there and stared into the darkness and listened to the waves, not for once did I think of either of them.

I felt oddly detached from my own world. It felt like Kanika and Roy were parts of a different world. Like they didn't even matter. I was happy where I was. Coming to Goa was turning out to be a good decision. Away from the rush of Delhi, near the nature and... the booze and the amazing sights, of course!

I turned towards the party and looked at it from a distance.

Just then, I saw a girl walking towards me. She was fair, medium height with blank black eyes. She was looking at me with a cigarette in her hand. There was certain looseness in her walk which suggested that she was really drunk. She was very slim, must have been around nineteen in age and was wearing a blue skirt with white flowers on it.

I saw that she was walking towards me, with an unlit cigarette in her hand. As she came within an arm's distance of me, she showed me the cigarette, as if she was about to ask for a lighter.

Suddenly, she bent her head and puked all over my shoe. I didn't even have the reaction time to pull my leg away. And then, she stumbled on her feet. Even before I could clean my shoe, I had to grab her from falling. I somehow managed to make her sit smoothly on the sand instead of collapsing.

"Are you okay?" I asked.

"Just take me to my room."

"Okay. Where is it?"

She pointed in one direction. Small huts had been erected all around the dancing area. As I looked at it, a thought crossed my mind – It must be a great place to stay.

I gave her support as she stumbled on her way to her room. Her weight was completely on me. I didn't like her smell. She had probably not showered for a few days. Her hair was undone. But yet, strangely, she looked pretty. Give her a bath, do her hair and give her a manicure. And she could model for a magazine. She was probably too slim for an Indian one, though.

She was a melody gone wrong. We somehow managed to reach her room. I took a sigh of relief after dropping her on the bed.

"Okay, good night then," I said.

"What?"

"I said – good night."

"Aren't you going to try to kiss me?" she said in a drunken way and held my shirt and pulled me towards herself. I was completely caught by surprise. I freed my shirt and took a step back.

"No, no. I am okay. I will take your leave," I said.

"But where will you go?"

I hadn't thought of that. Calangute Beach was a long way away. I didn't have the money for a cab. And I was pretty sure I wouldn't be able to trace Zeeshan at this hour.

I had absolutely nowhere to go.

"I don't know," I said, as I saw her collapse on her own bed and go to sleep in the middle of our conversation. Alcohol does funny things to people.

I washed my shoe in her washroom and came back to her room and looked at her. I liked the way it was shaping. And then, I switched the light off, and went off to sleep in a corner on the floor of that room.

"By the way…" I heard her shout out to no one in particular, seriously drunk. "My name is Navya Sharma and I am from Indore."

11
I need some Goa
in my blood

Next morning, as soon as I woke up, my thoughts went back to the previous night. I wondered if it was a drunken hallucination or a real memory. I opened my eyes and saw her lying on the bed. It was obvious that it had all been real. I got up and looked at her. What was her name? Navya, right? I sat up straight and tried to get a hang of what all had happened last night. I had a huge task ahead. I had to find out where Zeeshan was. And I didn't want to switch on my phone.

I walked up to the entrance, where a tall, French bearded guy was standing.

"Hey, have you seen my friend? His name is Zeeshan, he is smart—"

"Zeeshan? So you are Samar," the French bearded guy said. "Run to the Goa police station. And try not to come back."

"Police station? Why? What did he do?" I asked.

"Ask him when you get there. Now get the hell out of here," the French bearded guy shouted.

I looked at Navya's hut for a second before running to find my way to the police station. God only knew what Zeeshan had gotten himself into this time. When I reached there, I asked for Zeeshan. The policeman had the ugliest potbelly in the whole of Goa. He had a mole on his right cheek and had some random hair coming from the most unexpected of places.

"You know whose police station this is?" he asked.

I thought for a second. "The government's?"

"Mine! Neelesh Mesta! I am the senior inspector here. I run this police station."

"Oh. Okay," I said.

"How much money do you have?" he asked.

I honestly had no money whatsoever. If I gave a truthful answer to this question, I could risk trouble.

"Sir, the guy in the jail is carrying all our money," I said.

"You think he is still carrying that money, even after entering *my* jail!"

"Sir, please. If you can let me talk to him once," I said.

"*Bhai,* he has been arrested under the charge of prostitution. And he is not even giving his father's phone number. Give me his father's number and I will let you meet him," said Neelesh Mesta. He looked like the purest native Goan. He spoke like them and looked like them.

He was reeking of corruption and bribes.

"Please, sir. The guy in the jail would give you the money... Why drag parents into this?" I insisted.

"How much will he give me?" the policeman then asked upfront.

"Five thousand shouldn't be tough."

"*Bhai* jeans *khareedne aaya hai kya?*"

There was a long negotiation, at the end of which, we had to pay him twenty thousand. It was plain extortion, but we had no choice. Zeeshan withdrew the money from an ATM and gave it to the policeman. He had a very foul mood once we were done with the whole thing. Now that we were outside, it was definitely time for my flurry of questions.

"How much money do you have left in your account?" I asked.

"Almost none," he replied.

"And how did you land in jail, Zeeshan?"

His expression changed suddenly. He gave me a smile which could have meant several things. It could have been an embarrassed smile. It could have been because I had reminded him of something pleasant. It could have been because he couldn't wait to tell me.

"Remember the girl I was with, last night?" he asked.

"The red-headed foreigner?"

"Yup. We were making out on the beach and the police caught us. Undressed."

"But the policeman said you were charged for prostitution. So... you mean she was a prostitute?" I asked.

"Shut up, you idiot. She *liked* me!" Zeeshan said.

I considered the possibility. It wasn't really impossible in this wonderland of Goa.

"Then why did he say prostitution?"

"Because that way he could make maximum money. He must be doing it every day with random couples on the beach."

"Okay, okay. So where are we headed now?" I asked.

"Delhi. We have run out of money," Zeeshan said. "To Calangute Beach," he said to the cab driver.

I took a shower in the hotel and borrowed some clothes from Zeeshan. I hadn't changed since I had left Delhi and really needed it. Zeeshan gave me a blue T-shirt and black shorts. They were a little tight and hence uncomfortable for me. But still, I had little choice and I would have to wear them for just a while, until we reach Delhi.

Zeeshan picked his bag and we left for the railway station.

We had no tickets and no money. But Zeeshan was always confident that some deal could be struck with the Railway Ticket Checker. We might not have money, but I had confidence in his confidence. We had some cheap food at the railway station. Neither of us had eaten anything all day. We were starving.

We climbed the train and looked at the people at the station. Goa had been as full of stories as we had expected it to be. I suddenly felt like not leaving the place ever. I felt like staying back. Life would be a vacation! And then Zeeshan said something.

"So, looking forward to meet Kanika?"

He still had no clue what had happened. I realized I had done a great job of not thinking of her all day. But now that Zeeshan threw the question at me, for the first time it seemed to sting really badly. To begin with, the visual killed me all over again. Somehow, the pain was peaking high this time. I thought of Roy and all the good times we had had together. And then the betrayal.

My head was whizzing. I looked at the train and realized that I was heading to the same life all over again, where Roy would be my roommate and classmate and I would have to cross Kanika in college every other day. But then, I would get a good job, next year. And life would move on. It would be what it is like for every other person in the world. Education, career, marriage. If the whole idea of marriage was not scary enough for me, I now had to deal with Kanika's betrayal too. I remembered how innocent she had looked when she had asked me about marriage. The way she looked up at me expectantly, waiting for me to say that yes, I would marry her and her only. Was all that a lie?

Now when the time came to leave back for Delhi, it felt like stepping into a cage. I would have a life everyone else does. Boring, monotonous.

And to top that – without Kanika.

I was horrified at the idea. And then I thought of the previous night. In a dingy room on the beach, the gorgeous Navya had pulled me towards herself to kiss me. If I was to tell this story to people in my class, none of them would ever believe me. They probably never had experienced such a thing. And never would. And if I decided to go back to where they were, I was positive that I would not experience such a thing ever again either. The laidback, carefree, unscheduled life. The way you live like you want to live, without a moment pre-planned.

Somehow, the choice was very obvious for me. I got off the train, grinning stupidly as Zeeshan looked at me, bewildered.

"Where are you going? The train is about to leave," he said.

"I am staying," I replied, now smiling even wider.

"*What?*"

"I am staying here. This is Goa, the heaven. And I'm not ready to leave this place just yet. I need some Goa in my blood," I said.

"For how much longer are you planning on staying?"

"I don't know. For now, I am just staying."

Zeeshan was taken aback. I had done something he would have loved to do himself. The train's whistle blew.

"But you have no money…" he said.

"I'm sure I would be able to manage something," I said. How bad could it get? I was almost an engineer! I knew what Zeeshan was thinking. All his thoughts were focused on the possibility whether he could stay or not. But then, he did not have a reason as solid as me to make him stay. For all his outward aloofness and authority, he really did love Arshi and must have been missing her.

"Are you sure?" he asked.

"Yes. Absolutely sure. Are you staying back too?"

"I don't know… Though, I want to…" he answered. He was visibly torn between his options.

"Stay. We'll manage the money somehow. It will be fun!" I insisted.

"I know. But what if we end up with no food? We don't have any money at all…"

"Okay, Zeeshan. Whatever you want."

"I'm going back. Are you?" he asked.

"No, I have made up my mind. I'm definitely staying here."

"Are you sure…?"

"Yup."

The train left and Zeeshan faded from my sight.

People who had come to drop other people at the railway station began to leave. Five minutes later, I was standing alone on the platform, with almost no money in my pocket. A man pushed me from the back. I turned around frantically. He gave me an angry look, even though it had been his fault to have bumped into me in the first place. I realized I was nobody now. I was just a lonely guy who was standing at the railway station in an ill fitted blue T shirt and black shorts.

Soon, people who had come to drop people disappeared. And I was left alone thinking – What next?

12

A punch in the face

Standing alone at the Railway Station, I could think of only one thing. WoodStock Village. How do I reach there without a rupee in my pocket? I decided I will start walking in its direction. A few lifts here and there should make sure I reach there in a few hours. The best part was that I was not short of time. *All I had was time.*

People in Goa are always happy. And the thing about happy people is that they help other people. Somehow, three lifts and miles of walking later, I reached WoodStock after it was dark and the party had already started.

I was damn tired. I had slept not well for two nights now. The previous night, I had slept on the floor in Navya's room. The night before that it was the floor of the train. Add to that the fact that I had almost walked or sat awkwardly on bikes all day today. Every inch of my body was crying for sleep. At such an hour, even the floor of Navya's room seemed inviting for the safety that it offered.

I stood in front of the party area, where Zeeshan and I had stood just the previous day. I looked at everybody. My eyes searched for Navya. I went inside the crowd. I took around the whole party area. There were some one hundred people present. So it wasn't all that tough to locate her.

The first time I had met her, I was quite drunk and she was

as big a mess as anyone can be. And then, a very eventful day had passed. Honestly, the memory of her face was a little hazy. A certain part of me had been worried if my head had distorted her looks, in a strange way.

When I saw her, she actually did look a little different from my memory. I thought I knew the reason. One more day had passed since she had taken her last shower. She had just gone a little shabbier.

She was dancing with some Israeli guys when I walked up to her.

"Hi," I said to her, in the middle of all the noise of the African drums.

She obviously couldn't hear me. After struggling for one more minute, I signalled her to come outside the crowd with me.

I felt no sense of recognition in her eyes. As far as she was concerned, I was a stranger. It was more than clear that she had no recollection of what had happened the previous night.

"Yes?" Navya said, when we were at a good enough distance from the noise.

"You don't remember me?"

"Why should I remember you?"

"We were together last night. I'm the guy who carried you to your room," I said.

We were in a dingy corner away from all the noise, hardly visible to most people.

"Oh. What happened last night?" she asked.

"Umm, first you puked over my shoe. And then, you asked me to help you to your room and I did that."

"Then?" Navya asked, looking at me with a straight face.

"Then, I helped you to your bed and you asked me to kiss you."

"So, you kissed me?"

"No. I didn't. I said I can't," I said, defending myself.

Navya looked at me top to bottom and chewed on the thought. I had a feeling she didn't like the sound of the story

I had just told her. And then she said, "I'm not surprised. You look kind of doable. Take off your shirt."

"What? Here?"

"Yeah. Take off your shirt."

I took off my shirt, not really sure what she had in mind. Navya looked my body and then she turned around. She waited for a bouncer to pass by. And when one did, she went running up to him.

"Help! That guy there was trying to get touchy with me!" she said.

The bouncer looked at me standing topless in a corner. From where he was seeing, the situation looked very different from how it was. I didn't like the feeling as he walked towards me. The next thing I knew, he landed a punch on my face.

"Will you leave yourself or I will have to make you?" the bouncer asked.

I came out from the big gate of WoodStock Village, feeling insulted. I hated that girl at that moment. If only she knew how bad a situation I was in already. My right eye was hurting. I went to the beach and looked at the sky. And I let out a loud cry. I couldn't take it anymore. Crying out loud was my only redemption. The gravity of what I had done hit me in the face. I had no money left with me. I had no place to stay. I didn't know anyone in the whole state, where I was standing. I had nowhere to go to sleep. I felt a little scared. I was having second thoughts about having stayed back, already.

What had felt like freedom a few hours ago, then started to feel like pure responsibility. As if I had quit freedom rather than attaining it.

I decided to think straight and do only the sensible thing from there onwards, as I was shaken back to my senses. I promised myself to not act rash from then on and would not do stupid things that would make me end up in such situations.

My grumbling stomach called to me. I hadn't eaten anything

all day and was starved. I realized that fun and the party would have to wait for a while. First things first. So, to start with, I would have to concentrate on getting a place to sleep and getting some food to eat.

I went to the party area discreetly and looked for the manager of the shack. I had no idea what I would say to him but I did not see any other way of getting accommodation and food. Maybe we could work out some arrangement? I asked around for the manager and after a little searching, I found him close to the alcohol counter. My spirits sank when I saw his face.

He was the same guy who had told me that Zeeshan was in the police station. My hope disappeared. I saw his French beard and felt intimidated. He was a tall man with no hair on his head. The only visible hair on his whole persona was there in his French beard. He wore a ring in his right ear and was scary even before he opened his mouth, probably because he seemed like he was always angry.

"Sir, can we talk?" I asked, approaching him.

"Was there a hair in your food?" he asked straight away, without really looking at me.

"No," I replied.

"In that case, let me work. I am too busy right now," he said and looked at me. "What the hell do *you* want?" he said, once he noticed who he was talking to.

"Sir, I was looking for a job."

"Go home, son," he said, and turned around and left, as if I had never been there.

If he wasn't ready to even talk to me, then getting money out of him was a distant dream. I gave up instantly. My spirits were broken. Everything was falling apart.

I decided to walk to the beach. As I strolled out of the party and walked towards the water, I felt scared. What had I done to myself? Just a few days back, I was living a fairly comfortable life back at Delhi, with no worry on my head. And now? I did not have any money, clothes, nor place to sleep or even a little food. How did all this happen? I thought of the options I had but nothing came up. There was no way I could think of, that would help me get any close to getting any shelter or food. Defeated, I went and sat on the sand. And kept looking at people walking across the beach. Most of them were drunk, like I was the previous night. On some other day, I could have loved the serenity of the place. But a hungry stomach knows no serenity. It just knows hunger.

I took out my switched off phone from my pocket and looked at the display. I thought about Mom. She had no idea what all had changed in my world in last two days. If she was to see me in this condition, she would first cry and then slap me for having done this to myself.

A tear of my own escaped my eye. How could things go so wrong?

Sometime later, I managed to fall asleep.

I was woken up cruelly by a stick poking the side of my waist. I opened my eyes and turned around, but couldn't really see anything. The whole place was dark and my eyes were too sleepy. My vision took almost a minute to get focused.

"Wake up, idiot," I heard a firm voice, which seemed vaguely familiar. I blinked my eyes repeatedly to clear my vision and looked up at the owner or the voice. It was Inspector Mesta, the policeman we had paid very recently.

"Get up, bastard. This is not your woman's bedroom," he said, poking me with his stick. I got up quickly.

"I am sorry, sir. I was just leaving," I said, instinctively.

"I could see that. Oh, it's you! The Delhi guy, right?"

"Yeah."

"I know there is no point asking you for money. What are

you doing here?" he asked.

"I had no money and no place to go," I replied honestly.

"Look at yourself. You must be above 6 feet with such a strong built. And you say you had no money? Why don't you work, you bastard?"

"I tried... but I couldn't find any."

"Okay. Come with me then," said Inspector Mesta.

"Could you just give me two minutes? I will just wash my face and come?" I asked.

"Make it quick."

I went to freshen up in the sea water. I splashed some water on my face but didn't feel any better. It was terrible. The salty sea water did nothing to soothe me. Instead, I felt even more horrible.

I wiped the water away from my face using the sleeve of my T-shirt and went back to where Neelesh was waiting for me. He started to walk inside the WoodStock Village as I silently followed him. The party area was being cleaned up while some foreigners were lying around on the grass. I saw some of them showing more legs than they should have.

Inspector Neelesh approached the man running WoodStock Village. It was the same intimating bald guy with the scary French beard and the pierced ear. But amazingly, he did not seem intimidating in the least this time around. His angry demeanour changed into a pleading one, in front of Neelesh. They had a brief chat and then Inspector called me closer.

"You will be working with him. And do whatever he tells you to do. Leave your Delhi attitude behind. Any work is good work. He will give you food and a place to sleep. Rest is between the two of you."

"Thank you, sir. Thank you so much," I said.

"Never mind. This guy owed me a favour anyway."

"Oh. So how do you know him?"

"Whenever he runs out of alcohol during any party, he comes

to me. That's how I know him. And he is a nice man. Do whatever he asks you to," he said.

"Yes sir. Sure."

"And do not mess up again. I will not overlook anything now. He is taking you in because I am the one recommending. You screw this up and it reflects badly on me. And I would not tolerate that, you understand?"

"Yes sir, I do. I will do my best," I assured, still trying to figure out why Inspector Neelesh was being all generous towards me. Not that I minded.

"Good," he said and turned to leave, muttering under his breath. "I hope you don't let me down, boy. I hope I am not making a mistake..."

"Sir?" I called after him.

"What now?" he turned back towards me and asked.

"Can I ask you something? If you don't mind...?"

"Yes?"

"Why did you do this for me? I mean, you don't know me. And the only time you have met me is in jail. I don't think I left a very good impression... But you are still helping me out... Why?" I asked what was on my mind.

"I have no fucking idea."

"*What?*"

"Yes. I do not know why I am trusting you. I am just going by my instincts. I am taking a big risk by doing this. So don't you dare fuck this up. You don't want to get on my bad side," he said. And by the end of it, I was scared. I wished I hadn't asked him the reason behind his generosity towards me. That would have spared me the threat, at least.

"I understand, sir. I would try not to screw this up," I said meekly.

Inspector Neelesh walked away and I turned to face the owner of the WoodStock Village. The only question running in my head was – how quickly could I get something to eat? Because I *really* needed it to be soon.

13
Do Not Screw This

"Hi. My name is Samar Garg," I introduced myself.

"I am Joseph," replied the manager. He was suddenly intimidating again. "Can you read and write?" he asked.

I was a little taken aback at first. *Is he kidding me?* Until very recently, I had been a respectable student at a reputed college. The question was almost funny. If not for the situation I was in, I would have found it impossible to hold back laughter. But I could not blame him entirely either. If you were to see how I looked, after the turn of events since the last few days, you would have taken me for a poor day time construction labour too. Or maybe even a roadside beggar. Just that my clothes were not torn. Yet.

"Yes, I do know how to read and write. I was a college student before I came to Goa," I replied.

"Which college?"

"DCE."

"What do they teach there?" he asked.

"Engineering."

"Engineering? Are you...? Do you mean you are an *Engineer?*" he asked, looking impressed.

"Not yet, but I would have been one, after I finished my degree. Which I don't plan to..."

"You have not even completed your degree? Then what are

you doing here? Shouldn't you be in your college?"

"I don't care about college. I prefer being here. I like it here," I said.

"Okay, okay. But if I let you work for me, you have to know that you will have to do everything around here. You will have to take my orders and do whatever I ask you to."

"Hmm," I nodded.

"Today, you have to clean up this place. And after that, come to me. We need to discuss how things will work," he said and handed me over a broom and a bucket of water.

I looked at the broom and my only thought was – so I am not getting anything to eat before I work. My stomach grumbled in protest. But since I had absolutely no other option available, I picked up the broom and got started. I motivated myself by telling myself repeatedly that it was all about getting my first meal. That once I earned my first meal, things would fall in place. He would realize my worth, I thought.

I started the cleaning from one corner. I started with picking junk and throwing it all away. Then came – setting the furniture in perfect order. And then I wiped the tables and dusted the furniture. The Goa wind brings in a lot of dust. It worsens the situation quite a bit.

When I was partying, I had no idea that such a mess was being created. When I had seen a girl climb the bartender's table, I had never thought that someone was going to have to clean the marks of her sandals from the bar and pick up the pieces of the glasses she had broken.

When I had seen Navya puke on my shoe, I hadn't realized that someone actually cleans that place on the ground too.

When I had seen the foreigner shake up the champagne and open the bottle to celebrate some random football club's win, I hadn't realized that I would have to clean the thick layer of alcohol off the floor, to make it crystal clean, worthy of partying for one full night, once again.

And when I was the one doing the cleaning, only then did I realize how tiring the job was. If someone had told me a week ago that I would be cleaning a shack in Goa to earn a proper meal and a place to crash, I would have laughed at him. Even as I cleaned the whole place, I found it hard to believe that I was actually doing something like that.

All in all, four painfully exhausting hours later, WoodStock looked quite clean. And the part that I had been waiting for finally arrived – I could now ask Joseph to have a look if it was good enough for him. And if I had earned my meal, if nothing else.

Joseph came and looked at every detail of the arena. And then he looked at me with pleased eyes. I waited for what he was going to say next.

"Beer or whiskey?" he asked.

I grinned.

"Some bread," I heard myself say. "And something to drink."

I had a whole loaf of bread. I had never had so much bread in one day. It felt good. It wasn't oily. It wasn't heavy. It was delicious, simple and easy to digest. I had never relished a plain loaf of bread so much.

"Haven't eaten in weeks, have you?" Joseph asked.

"Just one day. But for the first time I haven't eaten for that long."

"But why?"

"College trip gone wrong," I replied shortly. I did not want to get into the details of the horrendous week I had had.

"Hmm." Thankfully, he did not prod either.

"Thanks," I said, after finishing my meal.

"You have earned it, son."

"Still… thank you for letting me work… So, you run this place alone?" I asked.

"You can say that. Along with a few employees, yes."

I made an expression to express that I was impressed. "I

think you have a great place out here. People must be crowding here every night, eh?"

"No. Not really. I make sure that I let in only a manageable number of people," Joseph said.

"Oh," I said, as I suddenly remembered how the place had been decently full the previous night, but not over-crowded. What I did not understand was the reason why he would sabotage his own business like that. I asked him so. "But why would you do that? If more people come, you will earn more money. So why don't you let more people come here?"

"See, I know I would earn more if the crowd here is larger. But at the end of the day, I'll get only what is written in my destiny."

"You seriously believe that?"

"Well, at the end of the day, we will get only what is written in our fate. Do you believe in fate, son?"

"No," I replied.

"See, a large crowd would also mean a higher level of maintenance and managing. And I do not have that kind of man power. So if more people come, and nobody has fun, from next year I get no money. We like to maintain a little exclusivity."

"Exclusivity? But everyone is allowed to enter the parties?" I argued.

"We don't turn down guests. But WoodStock is far away and not many people like to come this far. Plus, our parties – we play more of trance and psychedelic music – don't appeal to crowds who enjoy hip hop or trashy Bollywood music. So yes, we are exclusive."

I nodded my head silently. I didn't want to counter his years of experience and tell him how to do his own business. Joseph looked at me, as I sat there, with something akin to pity in his eyes. I seemed to have generated some feeling of compassion in him.

"You can take some rest now. Go sleep at that end there." He pointed towards the back of the shack. "People will start to come in only around 9. You can relax till then," Joseph said.

"Okay," I said. It was beginning to be dark. Just as I began to leave, I heard Joseph call me.

"Keep this," Joseph said, and handed over a few rustled notes to me which weren't more than a hundred bucks. By all definitions, it was my first salary. My lawyer dad must have pictured this scene a whole lot different in his head. It wasn't really the perfect setting.

And yet, I was sure that no other setting could ever have given me as much pleasure on attaining the notes as this one did. I grinned widely. I was ecstatic.

"Sir..." I started, hesitantly. "Sir, where can I take a shower?"

"Anywhere outside WoodStock," Joseph gave a cold reply.

I looked at the note and gave it a long, silent stare. I had no idea how I was going to spend it, even though I was sure I needed a lot of things. I needed new clothes. I could use still some more food. I could have kept the money for future use, but there just wasn't enough.

It might not make much sense, but I had a very strong urge to spend the money on the internet, by going to a cyber cafe. I wanted to check my Facebook account and my mails, just to understand how the other world was functioning, behind me. But I didn't want to blow the money away.

I went to the washroom and looked at myself. I felt shabby, unclean. I looked like an animal. I needed to become human before anything. And the answer became obvious to me. I needed a shower, before anything else. And I desperately needed to change out of my clothes. I went straight to a street side shop and bought myself a cheap pair of shorts. That is one of the best things about Goa – the cheap street shops. I do not remember my wardrobe having anything so cheap ever before. But even the cheap pair of shorts felt heavenly. I had bought them with my own money, the money I had earned.

I then went to a 'Sulabh Shauchalaya' (the public toilet) and paid for a quick shower. Never before had a shower felt so amazing. As the cold water splashed on my body, I felt more relaxed than I had been in the last couple of days. After the much needed shower, I changed into my new shorts and washed my old T-shirt. I then went to the beach and spread my washed clothes to dry on the sand. I sat there and waited for them to dry, but soon, keeping my eyes open started to feel like a lot of effort. My eyelids started to droop with drowsiness.

An hour later, I was in washed clothes from top to bottom and I myself was clean too. There was only one thing to be done now. *Sleep*. Finally. I didn't have a very good feeling about the place that Joseph had ascribed to me. I went to the back side of the shack, where he had told me to go. There was half a thatch, which was all the roofing that was there. There was a wall on one side and a beach on the other. The wind was blowing rather loud in that area. But still, the pain in my body didn't mind the place. In fact, the newness of it made it only more interesting. I could use some change. Imagine telling your grandchildren about this place.

I picked a gunny bag and spread it on the floor. The bag was pretty hard, but still, it was softer than the bare floor. I kept one of my arms over my eyes to shield myself from everything. The moment I closed my eyes, I was fast asleep.

Hours later, I was woken up by the sound of loud drums, coming from some distance. The party for the night had started at WoodStock Village, which meant working hours for me. The tables had turned overnight. From being a customer, I had turned into being an employee. I splashed some water on my face and started to look for Joseph. His face lit up on seeing me. He hadn't expected me to look so clean this quick.

"You cleaned up pretty quick, man. I was thinking you would be too dirty for good work," he said. I didn't know whether to take this as an insult or a compliment.

"What do I have to do?" I asked.

"Since you are so cleaned up, I think you can be a waiter tonight."

"Sure," I said. I knew I could be of better use than just be a cleaner.

"But there is another reason why I am making you a waiter tonight. I want you to keep your eyes and ears open the whole night. Listen and watch everything. The way people talk, respond, and react. What they like and what pisses them off. Keep your ears and eyes open for everything."

"Sure. I can do that," I said.

"Yup. Just be an observer for this week. And then we will see what can be done."

"Okay," I said.

And hence I began observing.

There were white people, black people, dark brown people, light brown people and some yellow people too. They were all coming in by the loads. WoodStock Village was the place to be – unknown to many and very exclusive.

And although being a waiter was a really tiring job, I actually had fun that night too. Apart from the running around, carrying people's drinks and rushing to get their orders, I also got a chance to meet a whole new set of people from a wide range of places. I got to observe how they reacted to what happened around them and how they behaved. And it felt nice. It wasn't like I was treated very well, but I wasn't treated exceptionally badly either.

So being a waiter was overall a better experience than the cleaning I did that morning. Until I saw *her*. Kanika. Just as I turned to get drinks for a German couple, I saw her. My heart stopped. My brain froze. I had no idea how to react to this. I looked at the tray in my hand and contemplated drinking up the beer myself. My blood was racing.

Before I did something drastic, I realized I had been mistaken. It wasn't her. It was just somebody who looked like her, from a certain angle. I had been doing my best to forget all about Kanika and that kiss, but seeing this Kanika look-alike brought back all the memories. And along came the pain. At first, as I saw her, I felt as if I was punched at the pit of my stomach. The pain was sharp and absolute. But then, realization dawned.

This was not Kanika. Kanika's hair was darker, longer...

This definitely was not Kanika. I sighed in relief. But the harm was already done. Even though I felt better knowing it was not Kanika, standing twenty feet away from me, it did not help the pain in any way. I was suddenly transported back to Delhi. My mind had the image of her from when I last saw her, kissing Roy.

All the efforts that I had put to forget all about her went down the drain. Only, this time it was even worse. This time when her thoughts came, along came another realisation – *I could never get over her*. No matter how hard I tried, no matter how far I ran... mentally, physically... I could never forget her.

I could pretend all through the day that Kanika Merchant never existed, but at night, when alone, it was her thoughts my mind was flooded with. When I did not have work to distract me and keep my mind off her, thoughts of her inevitably came to me. And memories of the good and the bad times we had gone through together. And then, the kiss.

My head was getting uncontrollable. I didn't know how low blood pressure felt, but I had a good feeling that this is how it must feel. I sneaked out of the party area, to take some time on my own. I went to the beach but the fresh air didn't make me feel any better.

I needed conversation. And there was only one name which came to my mind. Navya. She was one of the only two people I knew at WoodStock. But she had got me beaten up. A tussle ensued in my head that whether I should go see her or not. In the end, I had to decide between seeing her or going crazy. So I decided to go and see her.

It was around three in the night. I walked up to her room, with my heart feeling lower than it ever had. And when I reached her room, it was locked.

Fuck.

This was it. It pushed me over the edge. I was going insane. I had a whole night in front of me and I knew I couldn't get through it alone. I drank some beer out of unfinished bottles of the guests, and decided to fuck my duty and went to that corner where I had gone to sleep the earlier. I spread the gunny bag on the floor and closed my eyes. A thousand memories came flashing back.

That evening, Kanika and I were walking alone, on a deserted road at three in the night. We were returning from somewhere and we had chosen to walk rather than taking the rickshaw. We did that sometimes. It gave us more time to talk. And we never ran out of conversation. We loved talking.

The breeze was cold and pleasant. It could not have been more romantic and unsafe. Delhi, they say, is not a very safe city. I had planned an elaborate surprise for her in my apartment. I had decided this was the evening when I would finally tell her that she was the one for me. And she had no clue in the world about that.

I looked at her and I felt surer of my decision. And I wondered why I had waited so long to state something so obvious. I opened the door of my flat and turned on the lights.

Kanika stepped in and I waited for her reaction. I saw the look on her face. As expected, she was shocked. Her favourite wall in the flat had disappeared.

The wall was covered with small chits of paper. She looked closely. She noticed that every chit of paper had something written on it.

Kanika started from the top left corner of the bunch of chits on the wall. She pulled out the first chit and held it close to her face. It had the following text written over it:

It is okay. A pretty girl ditched me to go with some other guy. The regular. ;)

The message made no sense to her. She looked at me quizzically.

"What is it?" she asked in her bleak voice. She had had a long day. She was tired and winded.

"It is the first ever text message I sent to you, Kanika. And all these chits carry all these messages we have ever exchanged. I realized there could not have been a better way of recapping all the time we have spent together," I said.

I walked towards the wall and randomly picked up one of the chits from the wall.

I read the chit I had pulled. The message read:

This lecture is so boring that I would rather watch a Karan Johar movie.

We both laughed out loud on reading the message. Only the two of us could understand what that message meant and under what circumstance it must have been sent.

"I bet it must have been a lecture by Prof. Shukla," Kanika said.

And then she waited for me to pull up another chit to evoke another memory from the wonderful times we had spent together.

I pulled another chit which had more text that the others and read it loud.

Sex has three stages – Tri-weekly. Try weekly. And try weakly.

It was a forwarded joke which Kanika had once sent me in the early days of our friendship. It had obviously completely skipped our memories after all these months.

But today, when we read it, it was a laughing riot. We laughed so loud that I had to check my volume to ensure I don't wake up the neighbours. Soon, both Kanika and I were out of breath. A few minutes later, our stomach started hurting.

It wasn't just the joke which was making us laugh. It was also the cocktail of emotions we had gone through on that day. And then in the middle of it all, I had bombarded Kanika with all these wonderful memories. Both of us were obviously shaken.

Kanika went to the right most corner of the wall. She picked the last paper chit on the wall and pulled it off. Logically, it was supposed to be the recent-most message I sent her.

Kanika, I love the way you dress every day, as if you know that it is going to be a great new day. I love the way you frown and ignore every time the food sucks. I love the way you make me feel as if I am the least boring person in the world. I love the way you are interested in every piece of bullshit happening in my life. I love the way you want to talk to me, even when you have stuff to do. I love the way you make me feel like stopping everybody walking on the road and introducing you as the girl I would be spending the rest of my life with.

Kanika read the message and she was bemused.

"But you never sent this message?" she asked.

Just then, her phone beeped. She received the same message in her phone. I had sent it just then. Kanika read it once again. She looked at me with love in her eyes.

"I wanted to say something to you," I said to her, my voice exiting my lips and going nowhere but to her ears.

"What?" she whispered.

"That I love you."

The moment I said it, a gush of blood went through my body. If it shook me up like this, I wondered how it must have felt to her. Personally, I could have sworn there is no better feeling in the world.

"And I just don't love you," I added. "I lurrrve you. The word

love is just not enough. I need to invent stronger words to tell you how I feel."

She looked at me as if to confirm that I was not kidding. It took a second to sink in. But it did.

There was a pause. Every particle in my body was alert in anticipation of what she was going to say.

This was it. Years of meeting women, trying to understand what they wanted but more importantly, what I wanted, I had finally made a decision. I had managed to tell myself that this was it.

I had convinced myself that she was the one for me.

That was a year ago. We were so much in love. And that day, as I slept alone on the beach, I had no idea where she was. In fact, I wondered after what I had seen, did I even have an idea, *who* she was?

14
Like a Melody
Gone Wrong

I had no idea when I slept off thinking about her. The next morning, I got up hoping that I would get up with a clearer head. That was the good thing about being extremely tired while going to bed. That when you wake up, you feel so clear in the head. But my head was as clouded as it had been the previous night. Bad news. I washed my face and checked my body. It had absolutely no money. I thought of going and seeing Joseph. And I did not look forward to that. I didn't want to get out of my gunny bag. But I had to face Joseph sooner or later. He didn't look happy.

"Where were you last night, Samar?" Joseph asked.

"I was not feeling well. So I had to go and sleep."

Joseph looked at me furiously. But with an excuse like that, there was not much he could have said.

"This is the last time you are falling sick. Next time you fall sick, book a train to Delhi."

"Ok," I said, with my face hung long, as Joseph's anger hung in the air.

"So, what do I have to do today?"

"Same thing as yesterday. Cleaning in the day, waiting tables at night."

I nodded and went about my business. It was a damn tiring night. Kanika was now like a bad cold. She was like that bad nagging feeling which is always hanging at the back of your head. And the more I tried to get rid of it, the worse it got. To keep my thoughts off Kanika and the associated pain, I worked continuously throughout the night. And the trick worked. By the time the sun came up, I was too drained to think about anything. My brain was dead tired. It could not deal with stuff like bad memories and emotional pain.

The crowd began to thin as the sun came out and I had to serve fewer people. Tired by the night's work, every now and then, I would sneak an opportunity to take a breath and rest my legs by sitting for a minute. But then, someone would call me once again and I got back to running all around.

When there were less than ten people left, I decided to call it quits. I had never realized that being a waiter could prove to be so tiring. I looked for Joseph to tell him I needed to take off and take some rest.

"So how was it?" Joseph asked when he saw me.

"It was good. A great learning experience," I said, breathing heavy from tiredness.

"Great. Anyway, I was looking for you. We need to get the place clean. The broom is kept in that corner and here is the dusting cloth."

I maintained a straight face. After having continuously run around for the last 6 hours, Joseph expected me to clean the place once again. Was he kidding me?

Apparently not. He looked as if he was saying something very regular. As if, the fact that I would clean up the place was the most obvious thing ever. I got down to it, walking like a zombie now. My legs were aching, as if I had just completed a ten kilometre trek.

I picked the broom and a bucket of water, rolled my sleeves and my jeans up. I didn't have any alternate ones to change into if they got spoiled. I started to sweep the place. I caught my reflection in a glass door. Even to me, I looked like a poor sweeper. As if this was all I was capable of. I might have been a bit too tall and a bit too well built for it, but the broom in my hand was the most prominent feature at that time.

For a second, I wondered what my Mom would have thought, had she seen me like that. And Dad? He would have had fun telling his friends and business colleagues about his sweeper son!

And then I thought of what people from my college in Delhi would have thought of me. I could just imagine them laughing at me and making fun of me, mercilessly. Along came an image of Kanika and Roy, joining in the rest of them in their laughter.

Iron rod down my throat. That's how I felt. I tried to shake the unpleasant thoughts away and concentrate on the job at hand. But it had been an unusually bad night. Cleaning is a tough job, yes, but it does not require any brains. So even though my body was completely exhausted by then, my brain was still working.

Only sleep would have helped me keep my mind off the painful memories. It was strange how the good times hurt me so much.

All I could do was rush through the cleaning so I could retire to bed as soon as possible.

As I was cleaning, I reached the gate of WoodStock Village to throw away the water. I was feeling ugly. Just then, I saw a pair of legs walking towards me. They were shining brightly in the morning sun, under a short red skirt, which was flying around from the beach wind.

Tearing my eyes off the legs, I looked up and saw that it was Navya, coming with a backpack on her back. My spirits lifted instantly. I stood there and waited for her to look at me. We established eye contact and I kept staring at her. Compared to a broken person that she had looked like the last time I had seen her, she looked gorgeous this time.

Her long dark hair was in place, a few bangs falling partly

over her eyes, flying with the blowing wind. She was wearing a short red skirt which hugged her body in an ideal manner. It exposed just the right amount of skin – not so much that would make her look vulgar, but enough to make you keep wanting for more. Her white top was made for her. The way it complemented the curves of her body... You looked at her, and you kept looking. It was impossible to look away.

I smiled on seeing her and threw a 'Hey!'

This time, she did recognize me. On seeing me, she started looking into her purse. And she took out a ten rupee note and handed it out to me, as if she was giving me a tip.

"Excuse me?" I asked.

"You're the guy who cleaned my room the other day, right?" she asked, insulting me.

"Are you crazy? You didn't recognize me?"

Her demeanour changed.

"I did recognize you. But this is what you get for not making out with me when I asked you to," Navya said and turned around to leave.

"You've already gotten me beaten up for that," I said.

"But I don't think that's enough insult for that."

"Well, you've also puked on my shoe," I added.

She looked at me from top to bottom. Looking like a sweeper and being called one was not the best way to impress a girl. I wondered how much of the night she remembered. And what she had thought of me. But at least she seemed to remember that I was the guy she puked over. Good sign.

"Well, in that case, I think it is enough punishment," she said and gave me a plain, condescending look.

I kept the broom aside and we started to walk towards her room.

"Your room was locked for a few days," I said.

"Yeah. I had to go Bhopal for some work."

"Bhopal? But didn't you say you were from Indore?"

"I *am* from Indore. But as far as my Dad is concerned, I am presently doing a course in Bhopal."

"But you're not?"

"Not anymore. I didn't want to do it in the first place. So running away from there and landing up here is my sweet revenge on them. They don't know, of course. I will go back once the semester gets over there and tell them that I failed."

"So? Won't they be pissed about it?"

"They would be, but at least they won't send me back to that college," she said plainly.

"And Bhopal would be kind of boring, right?" I mused.

"Yes. And that is exactly why I am here in Goa and not there. Yesterday, Dad was coming to Bhopal. I had to rush there to pretend I had been there all this while."

As the words registered, I stared at her unblinkingly. She opened her bag and took out a cigarette.

"Lighter?" she asked me. I shook my head. So she groped some more in her bag and found a match box.

I looked at her. She was the kind of bad girl I had only seen in movies. She followed her heart and did everything she wanted to. And no sort of conformity seemed to stop her. She didn't mind breaking away from her dad. She didn't mind running away to her favourite party place. Not only did she make her own rules, she also lived by them. Navya was doing things I could have only imagined. Had anyone told me this story a week away, I would have declared it as fiction. Or maybe concluded that it must be some reckless hippie. But Navya was real. And also as pretty as she was reckless. And I liked that. She was like a breath of fresh air after the photocopies of females I had seen back in Delhi.

We kept walking towards her room, without any conversation. She caught me staring at her as she inhaled and exhaled the smoke of her cigarette.

"Since when have you been smoking cigarettes?"

"You think it is a cigarette?" Navya shot back.

For a second, I was bemused. And then I sniffed to check the smell. It wasn't a cigarette. It was weed.

I kept thinking of her story and trying to figure her out. She was so much intrigue, condensed in five and a half foot of gorgeous skin. I loved her independence. It was as if she had just decided that *Bhopal will be boring. Goa will be fun. Let's go to Goa.* And landed there, taken a dingy room in WoodStock Village and come to stay.

"So then, what do you really want to do?"

I am a boring conversationalist. Out of a thousand interesting things about her, I chose to talk about her career. She looked at me, as if she was weighing whether I would be able to handle what she was going to throw at me.

"I want to be a writer," she replied shortly, after a while.

"Writer? What kind of writer?"

"I want to tell stories which people will read and say, *this is so me.*"

We walked silently. I looked at her and thought about what she had said. She was so capable of being a writer. She had the courage to follow her heart. She seemed intelligent. And she was living an interesting life. There will be a lot to write about.

"Wow." I didn't mean to say that, but it escaped my mouth instinctively.

"What?" she raised one of her eyebrows?

"I, uh, nothing. I mean, I just think that you would be a good writer."

"Oh. You think so?"

"Yes, I do," I said, more sure this time.

I looked at Navya. Even though her face was as plain as it had always been, her eyes softened up. That was the thing with her. When she talked, none of her facial muscles seemed to move. Her tone did not modulate like normal people. Someone talking to her for the first time would feel as if she had no feelings. But as you get to know her, you realize she emotes only with her eyes. When I told her that I thought she would be a good writer, her eyes softened up, even though her lips did not curve into a smile. *There was definitely more to this girl than what met the eye.*

To me, she looked cute, even though not many people would use that word. It was as if what I thought about her mattered to her. Very soon, we reached her room.

"See you around, Navya," I said.

"Bye, Samar," she said. I turned, as she closed her door behind me.

She remembered my name.

15
An Arm Around Mine

Just as I turned after saying good night to Navya, I saw Joseph standing behind me. He wore a weird expression on his face. It was obvious that he had been watching the whole incident all this while.

There was a brief pause in which he gave me the coldest stare he was capable of. "You know what the first rule of WoodStock Village is?"

"No, sir," I said.

"That no employee hits on any of the guests."

"Hitting? I was not hitting on her, sir."

"Then what were you doing?" he asked.

"Just talking."

"Oh yeah? Talking, was it? Who do you think you are fooling? Do you think I am blind?" he suddenly thundered.

"I... sir, I wasn't... I didn't mean to..." I stammered and stuttered. Trust me, the scene in front of me was scary. A man who looks like Joseph is not someone you want to get on the wrong side of. Add to that – he was my employer; my only source of income. And if the way he looked wasn't scary enough, you should have heard him shout. It was more of a roar.

"What?"

"I am sorry, sir. This won't happen again."

"*Naah!* I am just kidding. For you, it is okay even if you hit on them. I don't mind," Joseph snorted suddenly. I didn't know whether to join in the laughter or not. I was still a little scared. He motioned me to walk with him.

We started to walk towards Joseph's room. He actually seemed in a jovial mood that day. We reached his room and this time, he actually opened a bottle of beer each, without even asking me. He tossed it to me. This was the first time in my life that I was going to drink at nine in the morning. And oddly, I didn't really mind. Alcohol might help me sleep better. We talked about a lot of stuff. About the women who had been a part of his life and the places he had lived at. His childhood in Kerala and what had brought him to Goa.

"So you love Goa, don't you?" I asked.

"Yeah, I love it here. I know life at this age can't be any better."

"So you can't think of anything you would want to have?"

"When did I say that? There are plenty of things I would want to have," he smiled.

"Like?"

Joseph shifted in his seat. He had been leaning forward until now. Now, he reclined back in his chair as if, he was recollecting a happy memory.

"I have lived here in Goa for the last twenty years. I love everything about it. I go home every summer and spend time with my kids. But every Christmas, Goa is busy partying and I have to manage stuff here."

"Hmm."

"So I wish for once to be able to back in Kerala and celebrate Christmas with my son. I have never had a chance to do that yet."

I nodded. Such a sweet thing to say. I started to admire Joseph a little more from that day. It was odd to see Joseph in the mood he was in. He looked nostalgic. It was like he had a picture in his mind, of celebrating Christmas with his son, but he could not. We students never realized how extreme the constraints of a job could get.

"And what about you? Anything you would really want to do?"

I hadn't expected that question. Once it was there, I realized I should have seen it coming.

I thought long and hard about it. But when I thought about my life, all I could think of was Kanika kissing Roy.

"I wish," I said, "I could go back in time and correct some of my mistakes."

Joseph hadn't expected such a negative answer. He had expected me to say something happy. He looked a little worried for me. He looked like he was trying to figure out what I was doing there. What had happened to me, to make me leave Delhi and run to Goa. But thankfully, he did not prod for answers.

I went to sleep at ten in the morning. The timings could not have been weirder. And yet, the moment I closed my eyes, I was enveloped by deep, blissful sleep.

I got up at six in the evening. It was the best time to get up. My body was well rested. And there were still a few hours to go, for the party to begin. I hadn't had a minute to myself for a long time. I checked my pocket – I had the fifty rupee note, Joseph had left with me with.

I knew exactly what I wanted that day. I went to the public toilet and took a shower. I had never been that desperate for showers ever in my life. Like most college guys, I used to go days without taking baths. But there in Goa, bathing had become a necessity. I could do with working as a sweeper. But I could not do with looking like one.

Plus with Navya around…

Anyway. I went straight, to take a shower and like always, I didn't have a lot of money in my pocket...

I started to walk across the road. I had forty rupees in my pocket.

At one point of time, I had been an internet addict. I had killed hours browsing profiles of random people on Facebook, checking and sending emails to random people and reading blogs which I liked. But ever since I had come to Goa, I had naturally left it all behind.

So that day, I decided to check my mail, succumbing to the addiction. But WoodStock was a weird place. It did not have many facilities. It did not even have a basic necessity like hospital, so finding internet was certainly frivolous. It took me an hour to find a cyber cafe and that too after I had come quite a long way from WoodStock Village. I walked into the cyber cafe and logged into my mail. My email ID had around thirteen mails sent from Roy. Just reading his name pissed me off. I logged out without reading any further. I logged into Facebook to check if anyone was missing me there. There were a few notifications. Some people had commented on my status. Nothing much.

I rued the money I had spent on the internet because had I not, I would not have had to buy the cheapest T-shirt I could find. It was the loudest shade of yellow. Had I seen anyone else wear it, in Delhi, I would have probably passed a comment or two.

I wore the T-shirt in the shop itself and looked at my reflection in the mirror hanging on the wall. I looked hideous. I tried to gather courage by thinking of the life I would have had, had I been back in Delhi. *This is worth it,* I told myself. Better life is better than better clothes. I walked out of the shop and realized that I had no idea where I was. All the shops and all the streets looked the same to me. I didn't even have the address of WoodStock written anywhere. I was officially lost as I started walking around directionless.

"Do you know where WoodStock Village is?" I asked a guy passing by. As expected, he had never heard of the place.

I asked a few more people. No luck.

Normally, I am a fearless person. But this time around, I felt a little rattled because if nobody gave me directions, WoodStock Village was a hard place to find. I could have roamed around the entire state of Goa and still would not have found it. I was getting frenetic. Just then, I saw a face. It was Navya. It was as if she was sent to help me out. She looked at ease, definitely aware of where she was. But I was too embarrassed to walk up to her and tell her that I was lost. So I decided that I would approach her and just start walking beside her.

I remembered the T-shirt I was wearing and walking up to her in that T-shirt was definitely not a pleasant thought. But then, I would never have found my way back to WoodStock Village on my own. I looked around. A few people there were roaming around shirtless. That gave me the confidence to follow suit and I took mine off too. I wasn't badly built so it didn't embarrass me. I wasn't sure how she would react on seeing me. We had had our rough moments. So I walked beside her and took her heavy bag from her grip. She seemed to need that – somebody to carry her heavy bag.

"Hey," I said, as I took the bag.

She turned around and looked at me, clearly taken aback. But she recovered rather quickly and came out with – "You?"

"Yeah. Thought you could use a hand."

She looked at me and contemplated saying something nasty. But then, it was more than obvious that she really needed someone to carry her bag.

"So you do loosen up sometimes?" she said.

"What do you mean?"

"I mean, you are always so uptight and upright when you are in the village. This is the first time I am seeing you a little relaxed," she said, and looked pointedly at my bare chest.

I thought of all the goofy times I had had back in Delhi. But all that seemed so juvenile now.

"Times change," I said shortly.

The two of us kept walking silently, as we thought of the next thing to talk about.

"So, what are you doing here?" Navya asked.

"I just came here for some shopping."

Navya looked at me top to bottom. She made a face and jerked her neck a little bit, as if she had had a thought.

"What?" I asked.

"Nothing important."

"I don't mind listening to the unimportant."

"Well, it's just that it's very hard to figure you out," she said.

"What do you mean?"

"I mean, when I talk to you, I feel I am talking to an educated Delhi guy. But when I look at you, you look as if you have come from a slum in Mumbai."

I smiled. I didn't know what to say to that. If she knew my story, she would have known the reason behind everything. But I didn't feel like getting into all that. I had been doing a good job of keeping my mind off Kanika. And I did not want to change that.

"My life is more eventful than the usual," I said.

We walked in silence for a while.

"I have a feeling you must have been very different in a different world. You do not come across as someone who was always like this. You must have been different..." she said.

"I sure was."

"Then what changed you?"

"Things happen, Navya. And a lot of things have happened to me recently. I needed a break from what I was," I said.

"What things?"

"Please let's not get into all that?"

She nodded silently, probably judging from my tone that I really did not want to talk about it. I sensed that she wanted to prod me more. But she did not. She was sweet.

"Anyway… enough about me. Tell me, weren't *you* a different person in a different world?" I asked.

"What do you mean?"

"I mean, weren't you just a regular college student back in Indore? Like everyone else?"

"Yeah, but I was never that person. I am more of what I am living right now," she said.

"Yeah. You look it."

"How can you say that? You haven't seen how I was back in Indore!"

"I know. But I can still tell. You look so much at home here," I said.

"Hmm. And you are not this person. You are more of that person you were in Delhi."

I smiled. I wondered what made her say that. I thought I would let it go, but I somehow could not ignore what she said. She had that kind of presence.

"What makes you say that?" I asked.

"You are way too smart for this place. This place is for people who can't cope with the real world. It's like a place people run to for refuge. When I look at you, I can see that it is a temporary thing for you."

"This is not a *temporary* thing. This is where I am going to be," I said, firmly.

"I don't think so."

"You don't know me. So don't judge."

"Okay, okay. Relax," she said, throwing her hands up in surrender.

We kept walking as we talked. It had been a pretty long walk. I had no idea that I had walked on so much to reach the market. In fact, the area didn't look at all familiar. I could tell that it wasn't anywhere close to WoodStock because I had started to know the area around WoodStock pretty well by then.

"I didn't know WoodStock was so far," I said.

Navya looked at me for a second with a weird look on her face. "You have no idea where we are, right?"

"Nope," I said, with a straight face.

"Why didn't you tell me you wanted to go to WoodStock? I thought you were walking with me just like that!"

"Okay," I gulped it in. "Then, where are we?"

"We are close to Anjuna beach. If you want, I can call you a cab to drop you back?"

I mentally counted the money in my pocket. The cab fare would be equal to my one week salary. It was out of the question.

"Don't worry. I will walk back," I said.

"Walk back? Didn't you realize we have come very far?"

"Yeah. But I will manage."

Navya thought about it for a second and offered, "Or wait, you can join us at this party I'm going to. My friends will drop you back when the party ends."

"Is it at Anjuna beach?" I asked.

"No. From here, we would be walking in the direction opposite to Anjuna beach to get there."

"Oh. Okay."

"Why?" she asked.

"No, nothing. Just asking," I shrugged. What I did not tell her was that I could not go to Anjuna beach. I had been there before. With Kanika.

"So? You're coming?"

"I don't know…"

"Come on! I would feel nice if you come," she said and gave me a brand new look. I concentrated hard to understand what it said. And then it struck me.

Voila! It was the 'please' look. I lost the battle to her that very moment.

But that would mean that I would have to take the night off from work. I thought about my options. There was not much to think, really. It was not like I had many options. My only concern was to inform Joseph that I won't be available for the night's work.

"Okay, I will stay. But I will have to make a call from your cell phone."

I called up Joseph to tell him that I wouldn't be coming for work that night. This was the first time in my life that I was making such a call. I felt nervous. For all the friendliness that we shared generally, Joseph was still a little scary at times. And of course, he still intimidated me sometimes.

But the call was more pleasant than I had expected it to be. He did not mind me taking a night off from work, as long as I knew I would not be paid for the night. I did not argue. In fact, I did not see a reason to do so. It was not as if I had any better option anyway. So I agreed politely and hung up.

"Let's go?" Navya asked, putting her arm around mine. After a long long time, my heart skipped a beat.

16
Fuck My Life

When I walked into the party, only one thing was going through my head – I didn't want to end up being the only guy without a shirt at the party. But as soon as I entered the place, I saw at least two more guys standing shirtless. I sighed and instantly felt at ease. It wasn't my natural self to go without a shirt to a party, but anything was way better than the brand new yellow T-shirt I was carrying. Especially with Navya around.

The party was a huge let down. All the guys were Navya's age, which means two years younger to me. Just two years, and it felt like a generation gap. Immediately, I felt out of place. Seeing them, I realized how Navya was so ahead of her age. So much more mature. Talking to her, I had never realized that I was talking to someone who had seen any less of the world.

I took a corner and decided to concentrate on my beer. Navya was busy chatting with the 'boys'. I sat on a stool in the least visible end of the bar and observed people around me. But I soon lost interest.

So I decided to observe Navya instead. She was trying hard to look like a carefree young girl. She was talking to everyone politely and mixing up. But still, I could see that it was all superficial. She was not what she was projecting to be. She was more of the kind who would prefer sitting in a corner with people she wanted to be with than socializing with everyone at the party. And yet, she was doing the latter.

One look into her eyes and I knew she was just trying to fit in and emote so that her friends would not label her as a freak. This was her struggle. To seem normal and one of the crowd. She was a mystery in herself. As I watched her talk to her friends, I felt that she had managed a soft place for herself, in my heart. I hadn't realized until now how big a part she had become of my life. She was my best friend. She was my distraction from everything I did not want to think of.

After a while, she noticed me sitting in a corner, feeling left out. She immediately started to walk towards me. She was too polite to not come to me and strike a conversation. She felt as if she was the host and wanted to keep me from getting bored.

Or maybe she just preferred talking to me over the rest of the people in the party. I smiled a little internally.

"Hey," she said, as she came to me.

"Hey."

"This party is dead, no?"

"Yeah, it is. Not much going on here… And I feel kind of tired too," I said.

"Hmm," she said. I knew her well enough by then to know that she was disappointed. She had so skilfully mastered her reactions to look genuinely interested in whatever everyone in the party had to say.

"What?" I asked when I saw the look in her eyes.

"Nothing… I mean, I was just hoping we will walk back to WoodStock. But if you are tired…"

"I will manage. Let's go," I was quick to say.

Her eyes softened up. And that pleasant look in her eye was enough to make up for the long walk my legs would have to face. Navya said bye to all the boys. And we started our long walk. I recapped all the distance I had walked in the evening.

My legs were going to develop cramps at the end of it. But strangely, I did not mind at all.

"I thought you were enjoying it," I said, though I knew well enough that she was not.

"I am good at pretending."

"But weren't all those people your friends?"

"They are. But then, they are just way too juvenile for me. Do you know what their favourite topic of conversation is?" she said and shrugged her shoulders.

"What?"

"Football."

I smiled and looked at Navya. She was so calm and so much at peace with herself. And yet, she was so mature, as if she has seen everything there is to see. I felt fortunate to have bumped into her. It was as if she was re-teaching me how to live. The time I spent with her invariably took me away from my worries and those painful memories.

It might sound odd, but – Navya was like a rehab for me.

"Aren't you feeling cold?" *my rehab* asked.

"Umm… I am, actually. Should I put on my T-shirt?"

"Why are you asking me?"

"Just like that," I said.

"Good that you did. Because I can think of a better option," Navya said, and she stepped forward and hugged me. More than the warmth of her body, I felt the warmth of her heart. It was exactly what I needed at that time.

"You are an amazing person, Navya," I said. And just then I felt something else too. It was an emotion I had least expected. I felt guilt. I wasn't supposed to feel this way. Why was I feeling guilty? Was it because of Kanika, the girl who had kissed my own roommate? This was just plain stupid. My hands must have gone stiff. Or my body language must have given me away because Navya sensed it immediately.

"What happened, Samar?"

"Nothing. Let's just go home," I said.

Navya didn't throw any more questions at me. As I said, she was way too mature for her age. And that is what made her so likeable and respectable at the same time. As we walked on, conversation was disrupted since that moment. We needed an icebreaker after what had happened and I was raking my head to come up with something. I did not need any. She did a good job of breaking the ice.

"It's my body odour, isn't it?" Navya said and gave me a naughty look.

I looked at her. The cuteness of her face and what she had said touched something in me. I promised myself that for the rest of my life, I will take great care of this girl, no matter where I am. This girl was special. I felt an urge to tell her what the real reason was. But then, it would change the way she looked at me. I was happy being an outcast. If I tell her why I was here, I would become a broken hearted romantic.

"Samar?"

"Yes?"

"When I hugged you... why didn't you hug me back?"

"It's the weirdest thing ever. Something I never expected..." I said.

"What?"

"When I hugged you, I felt guilty, as if I was committing a big sin."

"But why?" she asked.

"I don't know."

We walked on. We were both thinking why I had felt so.

"So, you like someone," she said.

"No."

"You're lying."

I couldn't think of a retort for that. Maybe, a part of me was still very much in love with Kanika. I still could not think of anyone else the way I thought of her. I never felt for anyone else what I felt for her. She had ruined me for life.

Would I never be able to love anyone as conditionally as I loved Kanika? I looked at Navya. She was young, gorgeous, smart and right beside me. What was there not to fall for? There was no reason why I shouldn't be in love with her. And yet, just hugging her made me feel guilty.

Fuck my life.

So this was how my every day was going to be. I would break my back by working all night. And then I would get a good day of sleep. And I would wake up and spend my day's earning in the evening. It will be my own little game. And it felt nice too.

I changed into my newly acquired yellow T-shirt, the one that I hated a lot, and went to the beach for a random walk. I did not get much free time, so whenever there was an hour off, I ran away from the shack and wandered about the beach. It was a lazy evening, and I could not see many people around. And that, for some weird reason, made me feel lonely.

I suddenly had a craving to talk to Mom. If I told her the truth about where I was and what I was doing, she would freak out. She would shout at me, I knew. But I felt like hearing her do that. I felt like being cared for. Though back in Delhi, her frequent calls bugged me to no extent, I missed them terribly then. I needed my Mom.

Just then, I saw Navya walking a little distance away from where I was and I ran for cover. After having come across in that ugly sweeper like condition once, I couldn't have faced her in that ugly T-shirt too.

Later that day, I met Joseph. That was another part of my daily ritual. When Joseph assigned me the task for the day.

"Hi Joseph," I said as I walked up to him.

"You're here. Good," he looked up from his accounts and said.

"Yeah. So what do you need me to do tonight?"

"You have to spend the night in the kitchen tonight," he said.

What? I was taken aback. After having battled it out for nights as a waiter, I was finally beginning to get a hang of it. "In the kitchen? Me? Are you serious?" I asked.

"Yes," he said shortly. He seemed preoccupied that night.

"But why kitchen?"

"You need to know everything that happens around here. So you should know about the kitchen too," he said.

I nodded, but I really didn't want to go. Joseph saw that.

"Come, I will introduce you to the head of the kitchen," he said, egging me on to come with him.

I had never been to the kitchen. And I didn't want to go there. I always wanted to be in the front. Show people my face and see theirs. I didn't belong to a backend place like the kitchen. Honestly, I would have rather preferred cleaning up.

I could hardly make myself go to the kitchen. My feet really didn't want to move. I was having a terrible day. I was wearing a terrible T-shirt and I was wearing it to a very depressing place. Just then, I spotted Navya at some distance. That made me quicken my steps. Before she could see me, I ran away to the kitchen.

"Here, meet the kitchen head," Joseph said, as a strong smell of spices hit my nostrils and a short, plump figure walked towards me.

When he came adequately close, some light fell on his face. I knew that face; I had met him before. He was that Thimpa guy we had met in the train.

17
The Thimpa Guy

The Thimpa guy's name was Thimappa Vajramatti. He was born in Hubli, a small town in Karnataka. His formative years were spent living the ways of a small town. He got used to it and accepted it as his lifestyle. When he was fourteen years old, his dad decided to move to Bombay. And Thimappa was admitted to a street side school, closest to their single room house. The street side school was the biggest nightmare come true for Thimappa. On his first day, he was approached by a nasty bunch in his class.

"So, what's your name?" the leader of the pack asked him.

"Thimappa Vajramatti."

"What?"

"Thimappa Vajramatti."

"What?"

"Thimappa Vajramatti."

"What? *Jhopad-patti?*"

"Thi-ma-ppa Vaj-ra-matti."

"That's too long. We will call you Mr Jhopad-patti."

The whole bunch went hysterical, laughing on hearing that.

"Where are you from?" another guy in the pack asked him.

"Hubli."

"You mean Idli? From today you are *jhopadpatti ki idli.*"

Thimappa knew that very moment that he would never come to like this city. Mumbai is that kind of a city. Everybody has to demand his space here. If you don't, the crowd just walks all over you without giving another thought to your very existence.

He came back home, looking for some solace from his father. Meanwhile, his father had been having his own adjustment issues. So instead of hearing his fourteen year old son out, who had broken into tears telling his story, Thimappa's father instead placed a full speed blow on his ear. Thimappa had never known this level of depression. The next thing he knew, he was sitting in a bus without knowing where it was heading.

The bus stopped in Goa, and he never went back to meet his parents. He never had many skills to do something big in Goa. So he landed a small job with Joseph. Ever since, they had been working at the WoodStock Village and made do with whatever little money they made.

Now I understood why Thimappa had guided us to this place in the train. Because he worked here. I went up to him and shook his hand.

"So you did manage to reach here. But what are you still doing here? Vacations got extended?"

"Actually, I work here now…" I said.

"What? But weren't you here to *visit?* You mean you now *live* here?" he asked, his gaze shifting from me to Joseph.

Joseph sensed my discomfort and came to my rescue. "Yes, he works here. Cooking, cleaning and other such stuff."

"Oh. But I thought you were a *tourist*. You don't look like you *belong* here…"

"But he does work here. And tonight, he'll be working with you in the kitchen."

Thimappa stared at us in silence, before asking, "Are you

serious?" He then turned to me, "Has Joseph gone crazy? Does he think you can get any work done here?"

"I am willing to learn," I said.

"He has to. And you have to help him," Joseph added.

Thimappa didn't argue with Joseph. He seemed like that kind of a guy. Used to taking orders. I looked around the kitchen. Apart from Thimappa, everybody else was definitely less than eighteen in age. It was very obvious how things worked in this place – Thimappa dictated terms and the docile adolescents followed his command.

He looked at me piercingly, as if estimating exactly how capable or incapable I was. After a brief minute's study, he seemed to have made up his mind.

"Okay, then you will cook pasta today," Thimappa said and took me close to one of the gas stoves. I was taken aback by his proposition. All this while, I had been scared that on the first day he would make me clean utensils or something. Making pasta was a stellar job role compared to that.

The only issue was – I had no idea how to. Brewing tea or coffee or preparing Maggi was something else. Those were things I could do. But this was different. Cooking Pasta involved a lot of complicated steps and was a long process. Add to that – I would be serving the dish to people in a restaurant, people who come to eat out. They were people who must be expecting the cook to be experienced and good at what he does. Not someone who was experimenting to cook for the first time.

I was screwed. I considered giving it up to doing the dishes, but just one look at the pile of dirty dishes sitting in the corner made me stick to the work assigned to me. And hence began the first cookery tutorial of my life. For all the hostility Thimappa had shown towards me before, he got quite friendly with me in one night's time. And I had to agree – he was one awesome cook. And an even better teacher.

The same routine followed for quite a few days. Six hours in the kitchen, working all night. It was followed by the cleaning. I still had to clean the whole complex every morning, as soon as the crowd started to thin. And then, my favourite part of the day –When Joseph would pay me the money I worked for.

He put his hand in the pocket and brought out two hundred rupee notes this time.

"But I don't have change," I said, since he never paid me that much. He knew I had no expenses, so he never felt the need to pay me anything.

"Keep it. This is more the normal rate in this area."

"So you were robbing me till now?" I faked fury.

"Frankly, I wasn't expecting you would still be around. I thought you would run away within the first fifteen minutes."

"Really? Why?"

"You don't belong here," he said simply and smiled. I did not know what to make of that. Navya had said more or less the same thing to me a few days back while walking back to WoodStock Village. Why didn't people get it? I liked Goa and I was there to stay. And no matter what they thought, I would stay. I would prove them all wrong.

But I hardly cared about any of that at that minute. I got double my regular pay and was thrilled. I looked at the note in my hand and decided what I would do with it. The call to Mom. Finally. For the last few days, no matter how hard I had tried, I had not been able to save money to make the call.

And once, when I did have the money, I could not bring myself to ring her. I did not want to lie to her. But I could not tell her the truth either. I decided to just keep the conversation short, so she would not get much time to shoot questions at me. I just wanted to hear her voice once. Just the thought of talking to her made me oddly happy.

I felt like hugging someone. But Joseph was not the kind of person who instigated hugging kind of feelings. If I really had to hug someone, Thimappa was my only option. So I went to the kitchen to look for him. His pot belly hung in front of him. He looked like a laughing Buddha with a moustache-less beard.

His apron was hanging on his tummy. His apron had layers of dough, spices and sauces. It was no easy task to hug him either.

"Seriously, even I didn't expect you would still be around," he said to kill the awkwardness.

I cleared my throat. "But why would I run? This place is more fun than you give it credit for."

"Yeah. It is. But it takes a little time to settle down. You know, when a man can say he is truly settled in this place?"

"When?"

"When he can buy his daily beer from his own money," Thimappa said and laughed a little to himself. "It's definitely a good place."

"Yeah. I would rather not live anywhere else."

"I don't know. Sometimes I feel like running away to Hubli and meet my childhood friends."

"Why? What is wrong with life here?"

"It's easy for you to say, Samar, at twenty one. What is your biggest aspiration? The hottest girl living in this cottage? At my age you have an ambition! A real ambition."

"So?"

"So to reach your ambition, you have to go to the city and make some money."

"Okay," I chewed on what he had said. "But why can't you make money here? I know some clubs are making money like crazy."

"Yeah, I know. Some of my friends are working in other clubs in Goa. And they are all filthy rich."

"Then what is wrong with this place?"

Thimappa paused. He thought a little about what he was going to say. "It's because Joseph doesn't want to earn money," he said at last.

"What? Why would he not want that? What do you mean?"

"I mean if he wants, this place can make loads of money. In the process, we will also get some extra. But he just doesn't want to make it big."

"But why?" I asked again.

"He has some stupid logic. That if too many people come in, we would not be able to take proper care of everyone. We will lose exclusivity and all that."

"He has told me about it."

"Isn't that the stupidest thing ever?" Thimappa asked.

"I know it is. But what can we do about it?"

"If I could get to run this place for a week, this place would earn the double of what it does right now," Thimappa said.

"Then why don't you ask Joseph to let you do it? You are his old loyalist. He might hear you."

"Ha! Look at me, Samar. I am pot-bellied, have a half haired head, with dirty looks. I smell of spices wherever I go. Tell me, if you ran a shack, would you leave it to me?"

I couldn't disagree.

"Then what can we do?" I asked.

"There is only one way, as far as I can see. He would never leave it to me. But he can leave it to *you*," Thimappa said.

"What? Are you crazy? He would never leave this place to me!"

"He will. I am serious. He really likes you."

"Why do you think so?"

"Because he is teaching you the *real* thing. You're not made for all this *jhaadoo pocha*. You're going to be the big guy."

Initially, I genuinely believed he was kidding me. But as we talked, I got to know that he was actually serious. We tried to think of a way to make Joseph let me run the place for at least a week. But we just couldn't think of anything.

With thoughts of finally getting to talk to Mom after long, I went off to sleep.

18
The Gift

I got up sooner than I usually did. When I had reached Woodstock, I had had no luggage apart from the stuff in my pocket. After that, I had bought some knick knacks like clothes. But all this while, my most valuable possession remained my phone.

I had switched it off in the train and hadn't turned it on ever since. But that day, I turned it on to make a call to Mom and turn it back off. I got a recharge done, with the money I'd earned, and switched the phone on. As soon as it came on, it started vibrating. It was Kanika calling. I thought of the odds that she would call as soon as I turn my phone on. There was only one answer. That every day since I had disappeared, she used to sit and dial my number repeatedly, all the time.

With a heavy heart, I rejected her call and called Mom.

"Hi Mom," I said.

"Samar! Where are you?" my Mom was hysterical. The moment I heard her voice, I knew that she knew that I was still not back in Delhi. She had probably talked to Kanika or Roy.

"I'm still in Goa Mom. Mom please, relax. I'm alright."

"Then why aren't you back till now? What are you doing there? We are all so worried for you, *beta.*"

"Mom, I needed some time here. And trust me, I'm

absolutely okay here. In fact, I'm having the time of my life," I said.

"*Beta,* I called up Kanika the other day. She told me that you've run away to Goa for some reason. She didn't tell me why but I have a feeling you guys are up to something strange."

"You don't have to worry, Mom. It's just that Kanika and I are not together anymore."

Kanika had been calling repeatedly all this while. I noticed I had received a few messages too.

"You two are not together? What happened Samar? Tell me everything!" Mom asked.

"I'm not telling you anything, Mom. Just trust me, I had my reasons."

"Tell me your reasons now or I'm taking the first flight to Goa."

When my Mom insists, one has to give in. So I told her what I saw, even though she absolutely refused to believe me.

"Samar, you're going back to Delhi right now, without any arguments."

"I will go when I will feel ready to go back," I said simply.

"You will never be ready, Samar. You have to go *right now.* And I'm not requesting you. I'm ordering you. You go to Delhi. Or I will come to Goa."

"Okay, Mom. I will go back," I said. I had no intentions of going back.

I heard my Mom sob. That broke my heart.

"I know you won't listen to me. I know you won't go," she said softly.

"Don't worry about me, please. I'll be okay."

"What are you doing, *beta?* Tell me honestly. Are you doing drugs—?"

"No Mom! I would never do drugs. Seriously, I'm okay here. In fact, you would be proud of me if you saw the kind of life I live here," I said.

"I know you won't do anything wrong. It's just that I can't believe what you've told me about Kanika. So, I just want the two of you to sit and talk once."

"It's too late for that. Just relax. Things are under control."

"Do you need money? I can get some money transferred to your account?" Mom asked.

"I'm doing a job here, Mom. So money is taken care of."

"You're doing a job!? Where? How much are you earning *beta?!*"

"Not much… Listen – I have to go now. I will talk to you later," I said.

"Aji sunte ho… Samar India me naukri kar ra hai," I heard my Mom shout to my dad in the house. I didn't want to talk to Dad. Explaining everything to him would be one huge task.

"I really have to go now. I will call you in some days."

"Ok *beta*. Take care."

"Mom?"

"Yes *beta?*"

"I… uh, kind of… miss you."

"We miss you too, Samar," she said.

I could almost see her smile glow across her face from the other end. It had been ages since I had said something like that to her. Never, to be precise.

But saying it then felt nice. And apparently, Mom also liked listening to it. She let out a satisfied breath as a nice silence hung in the air between us.

Just as I was about to hang up, she said, "Talk to Kanika once, *beta*. She has not been keeping well."

"Not well? What happened?" I asked, my heart beat rising instantly.

"Her asthma has been causing problems. Talk to her once. Maybe she will be able to convince you to come back."

"Okay," I said, just to end the topic.

We hung up the phone and I looked at my phone's screen. Seven Missed Calls from Kanika.

I switched it off and kept it back in my pocket. And my thoughts went back to the call. It somehow made me feel good. I stepped out of the booth and looked around. Since I did not even have a watch, I had to estimate time by looking at the sun. It seemed like I had a few hours free. I knew what I had to do.

I bought a black T-shirt and changed into it and went back to WoodStock Village. It was seven in the evening. My work was going to start at nine. I still had two hours to try my best to 'bump' into Navya. I kept walking around the porch of her house. I was sure that if she came out of her room, we would definitely strike a conversation. But the only question was – will she come out of her room?

I waited and waited and waited, scanning the whole area with hawk-eyes, fearing that I might miss her in the crowd. But there was no sign of her. I cursed my luck. Every day, when I had worn my hideous yellow T-shirt, I would see her around a handful of times. And when I was finally wearing something presentable, she was nowhere to be seen.

For the first time in several days, I was looking like someone who did not have to duck for cover every time a pretty girl was around. And now, ironically, the pretty girl I wanted to see was *not* around. Finally, my wishes were answered. She did come out at around eight. I immediately turned a little away and started to act casual, as if I was crossing her path absolutely coincidentally.

"Hey," I said.

"Oh, hi, Samar. Long time? Where were you?"

"Right here. You would be amazed at how busy things get in the kitchen every night."

"Yeah. But I have not seen you around in the evenings either…" she looked up at me questioningly.

"Hmm," I shrugged.

"Anyway, how are you? You look so much... cleaner," she said.

"Thanks. You are looking good too."

"Thanks. But I really have to rush now. I will catch you again soon," she said and ran out of the WoodStock Village.

And I watched her as she left. I realized that it was all I looked forward to all day – bumping into her and having a good conversation. However short the encounter was, I was still satisfied. After all, she would "Catch me again soon," as she had said.

And she had asked me where I had been since the last few days. It clearly meant that she had been missing seeing me around. I felt nice. I had seen her and had a small yet nice conversation. That was all I had wanted. And also, to not embarrass the shit out of myself.

The next day, Joseph called me up to him.

"Today, you will be the bartender," he said.

I was overjoyed. This was going to be the fun part. I thought a partial reason behind this could have been my brand new black T-shirt. I must have looked relatively more presentable that day.

"Here, keep this piece of paper. It has the recipe of all the drinks. You're an engineer, right?"

"Yes," I replied.

"Yeah, so make sure you memorize every word of this page before you start the night. But don't worry, you can keep the paper with you as you serve."

"Okay. Anything else I should know?"

"Yeah. I wanted to ask you, do you mind selling weed and things like that?" Joseph asked.

"Yes, Joseph, I do mind. I'm not going to do that."

"Okay, in that case, just tell everyone that they can take it from Toofan."

"Who is Toofan?" I asked.

"Don't worry about that. Just direct them to Toofan."

"Okay," I said and went to the bar counter. I kept the paper in front of me and kept looking at it and mixing the drinks. By 2 AM, I had memorized most of the drinks. The best part was that I was considered an equal by the guests. They seemed to want to talk to me. I liked the respect after the humiliating days.

The people there were humble, to say the least. Yes, there were some loud, trash-talking guys of my age too. But other than that, everyone seemed content with everything around them. They did not need their order served three microseconds after ordering, or their glasses refilled as soon as they took their last sip.

It was a relatively dull night. The atmosphere was relaxed. The music we were playing was slower and more romantic than the usual. We had decided to give the drums a break, judging by the lazy demeanour of the crowd. But that did not mean any less work for me. Yes, the crowd was not demanding light quick service from us, but we were still obliged to give them that. And it was a tough task. In the beginning, mixing drinks was fun, but soon tiredness came over. I had little energy left.

"Doing okay?" Joseph asked when he came to check upon me.

"Yeah, I'm good," I said and immediately replaced my dead-tired expression with a smile.

"Are you sure? You look tired."

"Yeah, I'm a little tired. Did not sleep much today…"

"Oh. You can take some time off if you want. I will manage the bar in the meanwhile," Joseph offered.

"No, no. I will manage."

"Come on! Look at yourself. You could use fifteen minutes off. And I like bartending anyway."

"Are you sure?" I asked, though all I wanted to do was find a place to sit and relax my legs for a while.

"Yes, I am sure. Here. Take this. And go find some hot girl to flirt with," he said and tossed me a bottle of beer.

I caught the bottle and took a seat at the front part of the shack. From there, I could see almost every corner of the place. But I couldn't spot Navya. And that was the only thing I wanted to see.

Talking to her somehow felt rejuvenating. Every time I met her, she left me with a certain calm feeling. And I really could use that then. But this time, no matter how much I wished, I still did not see her anywhere close. Thinking that she had probably slept early, I turned back to the bar. Joseph seemed to be having fun playing the bartender. I joined him and we mixed drinks together for a while, before he was called for some work. And that left me alone once again.

And then came Kanika's memories to haunt me. But this time, I was a little more successful in pushing them off my mind. The work-load provided me the much needed distraction too. And so, I concentrated at mixing and serving drinks. Some people chose to sit on the stools by the bar counter and seemed interested in making conversation. And since they were drunk, the things they said were interesting too. I got busy listening to them and giving appropriate responses to whatever bullshit they talked.

Bye-bye Kanika!

My hands were dead tired by the end of the shift. And standing all night left my legs sore. But getting rest was still a long road ahead. In the morning, I had to clean up the place like every time. I did it zombie-like. The physical labour was the only thing that kept my eyelids from drooping. Had it been something that did not require physical work, I would have fallen asleep right then and there.

Then came my best part of the day – collecting my money from Joseph. He did not seem in a good mood that morning, so I did not make small talk. I was too tired for that, anyway.

And then, finally, I went to the back of the shack and lied down on my gunny bag. I slept as soon as I closed my eyes. I was strangely content.

Like every day, that day when I woke up, the first thing I did was check my pocket. I realized I had more money than I normally did. All this while something Thimappa had once said had played on my mind. *You aren't really settled in Goa until you can afford your own beer.*

I realized it was time I bought my own bottle. I decided to go to a bar, and order a bottle of beer for myself. I took a shower as usual and went to the market to take a walk. I sat in a restaurant and asked for the menu. The best thing about Goa was its cheap alcohol.

But when the menu came, Navya's face crossed my mind. I had second thoughts about the beer and I got up. Next, I went to a store which sold ethnic Indian stuff. I did not have to search much. I saw a beautiful orange wrap-around skirt hanging outside it. It must have been around knee length, and had tiny flowers all over it.

I pictured Navya in it and she looked gorgeous. I went to the shopkeeper and asked him how much it was for.

"Three hundred and fifty," he said.

I made mental calculations. Three fifty bucks. That meant I could buy it in two days. I decided to do it. I would not spend at all for three days, buy this wrap around skirt and gift it to her. I was excited.

19
A Breath of Fresh Air

In the next two days, Joseph made me do a lot of things.
- One day, I went to the market and fetched everything the place required.
- Another time, I kept accounts at the billing counter.
- I then spent a day working on the gardening of the place.

Add to this, the stuff I had been doing before, and you would find the perfect blend of a multi-tasker in me. It was like there was nothing that went around the place that I could not do. I could cook, wait tables, handle the liquor counter, clean the place, tend the gardens, fetch stuff from the market, keep accounts and make calculations.

I felt like a labourer. I probably was one. Things were happening so fast that I could hardly keep an account of my own life. And I mostly loved it. Except the work which broke my back and dented my ego.

Sighting Navya was the best part of my day, even though I could not manage to strike a conversation with her. But she was the light of my day, the fire in my belly, the energy in my muscle. No matter how much the work exhausted me, seeing her just once was enough to make all the tiredness go away. She was like a breath of fresh air for me. She made me feel like there still was innocence left in this cunning world.

All this when I just saw her. For the two days when I was collecting money for that skirt, I never went to talk to her. Not even eye contact. I was happy with just looking at her. By the end of the third day, when Joseph was supposed to give me my money, I couldn't have been happier. I couldn't wait to see the look on her face when I would actually gift the wrap-around skirt to her.

"Here's your money," he said.

I took it from him and smiled. He noticed my extra broad smile. He knew I was up to something.

"You seem happy," he said.

"I just wanted to go out today. I was saving money since a few days and I have enough today."

"You want to go out? Why don't you take a night off then?"

"What? Seriously?" I asked, genuinely surprised.

"Yeah, yeah. We can manage for a day without you. You are not *that* important yet," Joseph said, with a smile. He was a sweet boss to have.

But then I looked at the money in my hand. After buying that skirt for Navya, I would not have much of it left. Could I really afford to lose my money for a night? I knew I couldn't, especially when I was gifting an expensive thing to Navya.

And I paused at the thought. Three hundred and fifty. Expensive. Just putting the two things together seemed odd. How things change! Back in Delhi, you would spend as much just on coffee without blinking an eyelid. And now, I had to pool my resources, saving for three days to get a skirt for Navya. And then, another thought crossed my mind – why was I doing it? I thought about that. I could come up with only one answer to that. *Navya meant a lot to me.* In the short time that we had spent together, she had started to matter to me a lot more than most people I had known for years. She touched a chord somewhere, and I just could not stop myself from letting her in.

"So go wherever you want to. Take the night off," Joseph said, and brought me back to present.

"Actually, I cannot afford to take a leave tonight," I said truthfully.

"I know you can't. But you don't have to worry about that. You will be paid for tonight too."

"What? I will be paid even if I do not work? Are you serious?"

"Yes, yes. I am serious," he laughed at my shocked expression.

"But why?"

"Because I am impressed by your work and am making you a permanent employee here from today onwards. And permanent employees get paid even when they have their weekly holiday."

"For real?" I asked. It was too good to be true. I had a job!

"Yes, for real. Now go wherever you were so excited to go."

I grinned. The concept of a paid leave hadn't really registered in my head. I was living under the illusion that I would be paid only for every minute that I work.

My excitement level was so high that I could have punched the air or something. My tiredness disappeared instantly. Just then, I got an idea.

Why not go to the market and buy the wrap around skirt right now? Why wait till the evening? The excitement will not let me sleep anyway.

So, that decided, I went to the shop and bought the orange skirt immediately. I held it in my hand and went off to sleep.

And then came the difficult part. Actually bumping into her and handing it over to her. When I took a shower and went to her room, I found it locked. Come on, this couldn't be happening! After so much build up for this meeting, she couldn't spoil it all by being out all evening.

I turned around to leave and almost bumped into someone. It was her. Navya was standing behind me, looking a little amused. I knew the reason behind her amusement – I had been standing at her door, staring at it as a kid would stare at a cake he could not have.

"Looking for someone?" Navya asked, throwing her head back and looking at me.

"Yes. You," I said.

"Good. Why haven't I seen you around recently?"

"I was busy getting a gift for you."

"Gift?" she asked.

I took out the skirt from the cover in my hand and gave it to her. She looked at it, top to bottom, with a bemused look on her face. And then she looked at me. And then I finally saw what I thought I would never see in this life. Navya laughed. I swear she did. It was a full blown, a loud laugh.

As her teeth glistened in the sunlight falling on her, I ogled at her without blinking. It was a breath-taking sight indeed. And that was when I realized – I had never seen her laugh before. It was the first time that she was actually doing that. In all the time that I had known her, she hadn't even so much as smiled. But when she did laugh, that day, I realized how amazing she looked.

"Couldn't you find a worse skirt in the whole of Goa?" she said, as she caught her breath in between the laughter.

She did not like it. In fact, I was sure she close to hated it. Technically, I should have been sad. She had out rightly rejected the gift I had brought for her after working so hard. But her laugh was just so charming that I couldn't let my spirits fall.

I grinned like an idiot.

"Come, we will go out for dinner," she said.

I had exactly twenty bucks in my pocket. The best I could afford was to take her out for coffee with some Parle-G biscuits. And it showed on my face.

"Don't worry. I will pay. Give me a second," she said and went inside her room.

I waited outside for her to come. And when she did, my jaws dropped. She looked absolutely stunning. Even though she wasn't conventionally pretty, with kohl in her eyes and those lips on her face, she could take any heart away. *Don't stare at her legs,* I told myself. I simply could not take my eyes off her. Not that I wanted to, but I was sure that even if I had tried, I would have failed miserably. And most importantly, she was smiling today.

"You're smiling," was the first thing I said to her.

"I have to. Otherwise the dress doesn't look good," she said.

"Let's go, then," I said, smiling softly. She had seen me look at her the way I was. I don't think I needed to officially compliment her. We walked out and she hailed a cab. It was all going to be paid by her. It was too good to be true. The night was shaping much better than I had imagined it would. It would have been much better though, had she liked the gift I had given her.

Once we were in the cab, I felt the pressure to strike a conversation. But I did not need to think of anything. She initiated the conversation.

"So you don't mind spending so much time with me?" Navya asked.

"*Naah!* Time is the only thing I have in abundance."

"You really speak like a writer sometimes."

"It's easy to speak like a writer. But it's more important to think like one," I said.

"Hmm."

There was a short pause in which I thought about what I had said. *It's easy to speak like a writer. But it's more important to think like one.* Pretty heavy, even by my philosophical-mode standards.

"So how come you thought of bringing me a gift today?" she asked.

"I just wanted to do something for you," I said.

"I hope you know you are not getting a blow job from me in return."

"Shit," I joked.

She smiled and came forward and gave me a hug. "I cannot recall when was the last time anyone brought a gift for me, without any selfish motive."

"Maybe this hug was my selfish motive."

"If that's the case, then I don't mind. It's actually kind of sweet."

I smiled. This was the best thing about Navya. She said what she felt. And whatever she said was always so genuine that you simply had no defence against it. Sometimes, when I talked to her and said something funny, she would suddenly say "you're cute", leaving me with no response. All I could do was smile. And I liked the fact that it was because of her. She was special.

The driver kept driving. I wasn't very familiar with roads in Goa, but Navya seemed to know where we were going. It was hardly surprising, considering she considered Goa as her real home or something. Who runs away from home and hides in Goa? She did. So she obviously was in love with the place.

A little later, when we reached Anjuna Beach, I was caught off guard. When in the cab, I had no clue where we were headed. But as soon as I stepped out of it, it took me about two seconds to decipher where we were. I remembered every detail of the place.

Anjuna Beach brought back happy memories which had then turned into painful ones. Just the previous year, when I had visited the place with Kanika and danced my heart out, I had loved it. Things were different this time. There was no Kanika by my side. I waited for the pain. But none came. I was amazed by the way I had inured to any feelings about her. Although the memories did come back, I somehow didn't feel sad. I didn't even miss her. Was this the new me? Had I finally gotten over her? Was this finally happening?

I felt good about it. This was how I wanted it to be. I had needed to get over her.

I looked at Navya and felt a little lost in her beauty. But it wasn't all about her beauty. It was more about her beauty combined with her tactless wit and the way she was loaded with intrigue. She held my hand and pulled me inside a restaurant. We ordered our drinks and she looked up at me and smiled. I smiled back. I wanted to get drunk. And I wanted her to get drunk with me.

And so, the rounds of drinks started. There was not much talking. We just concentrated on getting sloshed. As soon as we crossed the threshold of being called tipsy, I asked her for a dance.

She gave me her hand. We went to the dance floor and started swaying together. And then, there was a brief eye contact between us. I clearly saw Navya's head move forward. I had known that this moment will come, sooner or later, when I would have to decide whether I could kiss Navya or not. Every time, I had postponed the decision until this moment, when I would *absolutely* have to decide, whether I could kiss her or not.

I saw her head move closer, and before I could come to a decision, I felt her lips touch mine. I didn't move. I didn't kiss her back. I couldn't. My head was clouded with what was happening. I pulled my head back. The decision had been made. I still didn't have it in me to kiss her back.

Navya gave me a blank look, but she wasn't surprised. It was as if she had known that sooner or later, I would pull my head back, with a jerk. She seemed to know everything I ever did, as if I did not have it in me to surprise her.

Our heads were touching each other, even though we had stopped kissing. I looked at the look in her eyes. I had no idea what it meant. We had just kissed. But I didn't see anything in her dark blank eyes. It was as if she was closing herself from me. Usually, I was the only person she did not pretend in front of. But this time, she was not letting me in either.

It was not a nice feeling. But I decided to let it go. What we had done just then was enough to make up for the blank look in her eyes. I found no reason to complain.

"You will be a good writer," I said.

"Where did that come from?"

"I don't know. I basically mean you'll be good at whatever you will do."

"Well… I write a lot. But I have never let anyone read my stuff yet."

"Why not?"

She shrugged.

"What do I have to do to read what you write?" I asked.

"You just have to smile and ask."

"That would be enough?"

"Try," she winked.

"Ms Navya Sharma, can I please, please, please have the pleasure of seeing your best talent?" I asked, smiling.

"You can. But I thought you wanted to see my writings."

"What do you mean?"

"You said you want to see my best talent. Writing is not my number one talent," she said.

"Then what is?"

"I'll tell you when the time comes," Navya toyed with me.

She needed some pestering but I managed to break through her defences this time.

"Have you ever seen the paintings on every wall of WoodStock Village?" she asked.

"Don't you dare tell me that you painted them!" I said.

She gave a look which was her equivalent of a smile.

"How can you possibly be so talented at this age?" I asked, a little exasperated.

"I don't know. I just believe art is overrated."

"There. Again, you are talking like a writer. Saying stuff that I just don't understand."

"I mean most things are easier than you expect," she said.

"It's easy for you to say. You can say that because you are good at painting."

"No. I can say this because I truly believe that all this is not a big deal. Like even though no one has ever read my writings, I know what I write is good."

"Hmm. I used to wonder what you do all day, living in Goa," I said.

"I paint. And I write."

I looked at her. And I wondered if I knew her at all. She was a mysterious girl who seemed to have so many layers that you could just not know her. Every time I felt I was close to figuring her out, she did or say something to make her realise I did not know her at all. It was an experience in itself – getting to know her.

"Will you teach me how to paint?" I said.

"Seriously? That was the best you could come up with? You could find a better excuse to spend time with me," she said, as she looked at me condescendingly. Her kohl filled eyes gave her the fierce look she had intended. Yet, I found it hardly intimidating. In fact, it only made her look cuter.

"Can I pretend to learn painting and spend time with you?" I asked next.

"I don't mind. Just that I don't think painting is your kind of talent."

"Then what is?"

"I'll tell you when the time comes."

She thought about something for a minute.

"You should try your hand at writing."

"You think I can write?" I asked.

"Totally. It's easy being a writer. All you have to do is lead an interesting life and have some brains. You're pretty good at both."

"I never thought about doing something like that."

"Well, you could think now," she said simply.

"It is not all that easy. What would I even write?"

"Whatever you want to."

"Fine. I'll ask you – What do *you* think I should write?" I asked.

"If I was in your place, I would write a series of books, each one inspired by one year of my life."

"No offense to you, but – That is the stupidest thing I have ever heard," I said.

"But if you do that, I would love to read them," she said sweetly.

"I'll let you know if I do."

The next evening, after getting my sleep, as I walked out of my room, I looked all around for Navya. It was weird. The first thing I thought of after waking up was her. Somehow, meeting her was the part of the day I looked forward to the most. Being with her was strangely refreshing. As I said before – she was my rehab.

And that was what was even stranger. My days had started to revolve around my meetings with her. She had that kind of power on me. It was like there was a physical force pulling me towards her. And that was when I was just starting to know her. Man, was she hard to understand! When you looked at her, you would see a young pretty girl, who probably knew nothing about life and its bitter realities. And then when you talk to her, you might get a hint that she was a little more mature than you thought.

But it was only when you got to know her that she would

start to really confuse you. One minute, she would be like a girl with blank eyes, staring at nothing, with a distant look on her face. She seemed to have seen a lot more than you initially gave her credit for. Her innocence just stole your heart away.

Then – the words she said. She would look at everything as a writer would and say things that would leave you thinking. *"You are not over Kanika." "You are more of the person you were in Delhi." "You should try your hand at writing."*

And of course – Art. She was a true artist. She was a good dancer. She painted amazingly and I was sure she was a good writer. Hell! She even kissed like an artist! I would not be amazed if I someday find her playing a guitar in a downtown restaurant, singing a Heavy Metal song. Possible. I would take an eternity to get to know her, I knew. And it would be one hell of a journey. The best thing about Navya was that you never get bored with her around. She always had something interesting to do or say. Even if she was sleeping, just staring at her would keep you entertained.

After searching for her a little, I saw her next to the wall on the Western side. As I walked up to her, I noticed that she had a paint brush in her right hand and a bottle of beer in the left. Her hair was tied roughly at the back and her clothes were shabbier than the usual.

Her attitude shouted *I-don't-give-a-fuck*. It was like she was barely tolerating whatever was going around her. Though she never looked irritated, she always wore an expression that gave out a clear message that said – *Mind your own fucking business.* In politer words – *Live and let live.* She did not really care about many things. It was like most things did not matter to her.

I reached her and looked at the painting. It was a distorted version of Goddess Durga. Normally, Goddess Durga is supposed to look scary. But that day, she looked gorgeous, when Navya painted her. It was as if she had taken away the rage in her and replaced it with softness. And even though the image was mythological, the bright colours made it seem trendy and kind of cool.

"It looks nice," I said.

"Oh, hey Samar! When did you come? You slept well?" she asked, smiling widely at me. She seemed genuinely happy. I hoped it had something to do with seeing me.

"Hi. I just came. And yes, I slept well."

"Cool. You saw my painting?" she asked and motioned to the Goddess Durga painting. "How does it look?"

"Amazing. Like really. Out of the world."

"It does? I hope it doesn't make this place look like a temple."

"It isn't. It's looking like a youngsters' take on Goddess Durga," I said.

"That is exactly how I wanted it to be," she said.

"You look good when you smile" I said, changing the topic.

Navya looked at me. For years, people had told her she didn't smile. She had accepted herself as a person who just couldn't smile. And now, somebody had seen her smile and even complimented her. It was something rather new for her.

"What are you doing to me, Samar?"

"What?"

"You've started making me smile... You're changing me."

"It's a good change, Navya. Be happy. Why didn't you smile earlier?"

"It's not like I don't want to smile. But I just didn't find anything worthy of it."

There was an unusual twinkle in her eye that day. So this was what excited her. Rest everything was way too predictable for her. This is what you had to do to excite her. Pass a simple, but genuine compliment to her work.

And then we got into a boring discussion about her colours and her creative process. I wasn't really interested, but I needed to do it to justify my presence there. So I did not even listen to what she said. No, what I mean is – I saw her lips move and I heard her voice, but I did not make sense of her words. I was content with just looking at her.

She looked cute. Not that she did not look cute every other day, but she was looking exceptionally so that day. I knew it had something to do with what she was talking about. She really was very passionate about painting. I had never seen anyone talk so enthusiastically about colours.

And I knew I should be listening to her, but I was not. I agree that what she was saying must have been interesting too, but the extra excitement in her voice and the glitter in her eyes were new to me. And that was why they had my undivided attention. My eyes saw her talk animatedly and my ears heard her happy voice. She went on for a while and I continued to stare at her. Once she was done, she stretched her arms. I could see that she was tired.

"You want me to help you take this stuff to your room?" I offered automatically.

"Yeah, please. That's your tuition fee," she said.

I picked her stuff and we started to walk towards her room. The last time I had come to that room, it had been a regular room like any other at WoodStock. With basic stuff in it, no frills. But that day, I saw her room's walls covered with paintings all over it.

And then, I saw something that took me aback. I had not seen it coming. On the wall right opposite the entrance, I saw a sketch of a guy without a shirt. I looked at the painting closely and I knew there was something *odd* about it. I walked a little closer and tried to guess what it was. And then it struck me. The guy's face was somewhat like mine. Navya had sketched how I would look topless. Same eyes, same nose, same lips, same face cut. But the sketch was unfinished, so it was hard to be sure.

"Is that me?" I asked.

"Yeah."

"Can I ask why?"

"You were looking good that day, when we went to party and you were shirtless," she stated simply, not in the least embarrassed that she was sketching me.

I looked at her. The compliments must have been in my eyes, because I saw her look amused, yet again, within a span of two hours. It was a rarity because this was a different kind of a look. It reached her eyes, and along with the twinkle, it was priceless.

"You are genuinely talented," I said.

"Thanks."

"You should so do this professionally."

"No, no. This is just for time-pass. I would rather become a writer," she said.

Her beer was still in her hand. I wondered how much a factor was beer behind her being so amused. If it was enough to make her behave so differently, she must be at least a few bottles down. I liked this version of her.

"I should go. You must be tired," I said.

"Yeah, a little. But..."

"But?"

"Why don't you stay?" she asked sweetly.

I looked at her. I had no idea what she meant. Was she getting naughty with me? One thing I knew about Navya was that she wouldn't want me to take the lead. I was just supposed to follow her lead, as she would guide me to whatever she would.

I nodded silently. She smiled and pulled me to her bed. But even though she was a little drunk, alcohol did not make her lose her senses. She came close to me, pecked me on my cheek and shifted back to rest her head on the bedpost. That way, we were at opposite ends of the bed.

"Samar..." Navya said.

"Yes?"

"Sometimes, even I feel like talking," she said.

"Okay… I am listening."

"Sometimes I wish I had a strong shoulder I could bank on."

"That is so corny. Also, that is so unlike you," I said truthfully. It was weird to see Navya like that, to say the least. I had never seen her talk like that. It was as if I was seeing a whole different dimension of her.

"I know. I know I don't talk like this. Ever," she said.

"But I want to hear you talk like this," I said.

She studied my expression, probably to judge whether I was serious or just making fun of her. She seemed to come to a conclusion. And then, she smiled.

"Yeah, so I was saying, sometimes I wish I could throw my arms around a broad body like yours," she said, coming to my side of the bed and sitting next to me. She then crept her arm around me and half hugged me. I held her. I was all ears.

"Can I tell you something I have never said to anyone?" she said.

"Hmm."

"I think you are kind of handsome."

"Kind of?"

"Yeah. Kind of."

"Thanks," I said. "Can I tell you something?"

"Sure."

"I feel I don't know you at all."

"What do you mean?"

"I mean – I feel there is so much more to you than I know. As if you don't tell the whole thing when you talk to me."

"I know what you mean," she said. I waited for her to say more, but she did not. And I did not prod either.

We were both lost in our individual thoughts. We weren't

really drunk. But the alcohol and the random talk had left us happy high. It was a pleasant feeling.

"One more thing, Samar."

"Yes?" I asked.

"I am falling for you."

I stayed silent. For no explicable reason, I wasn't really surprised, even though Navya had never dropped even a shadow of a hint until now.

"Okay," I said.

"Are you falling for me too?"

I compared what I felt for Navya to what I had felt for Kanika. And I knew the answer. There was no comparison. I was definitely not in love with Navya. Even though I barely even thought of Kanika, she was what would always rule my heart, I knew. Her memories no longer haunted me, but they had not completed left me either. She had ruined me for everyone else. Even Navya.

I turned to look at her. Navya was special. She was who I waited for all the time. She was who I wanted to talk to. She was the one I thought about unceasingly. But she was not someone I loved. It was like even though Kanika had left my life, she still had all of my heart. There was no space for anyone else there.

"I am not, Navya," I said.

"Okay."

There was silence for quite some time.

"But then we can't be friends," Navya said.

"Why?"

"It never works. It never has, it never would. Someone would eventually get hurt. Most probably – Me."

"Oh come on! What kind of stupid logic is that?" I protested.

"It is just an axiom which I truly believe in."

"Okay. What should we do then?"

"We should go our separate ways," she said casually. Painfully casually.

"I don't think there is any need for that."

"It's easy for you to say that," she said.

"Are you sure we need to do this?"

"Yes. We just *have* to go our separate ways."

"Okay," I conceded. And turned around and hugged her tighter.

"But I don't want to go. I don't think I am strong enough to let you go. If you ask me to stay sweetly, I might stay back," she said and hugged me tightly. She wasn't really hugging. She was just holding me with all her strength.

I sighed in relief. Just the thought of life without Navya shook me up a little. Quite frankly, she was what I was living for then. If she had left me suddenly, I had no idea what I would have done. I would have had no one to even talk to. If anything, I was dependent on her. And just because I did not love her, did not mean she was not special to me. She was, and a lot more than everyone else in the world. But even if I tried, I could not fall in love with her. Kanika had messed with my heart big time.

I was being selfish, by wanting her to stay. And I knew that it would be hard for her – to love me and know that I would never love her back... that I would always love Kanika. But I could not let her go. I could not exist without her.

"Stay," I murmured into her ear.

20

What You Can Never Have

I made my way out of the shack, lost in thoughts. Joseph had asked me to fetch some stuff for kitchen and I was mentally calculating our budget. It was a comparatively easier task. I got to the store and gave the shopkeeper my list.

"I have come from WoodStock Village. Joseph must have talked to you?" I asked.

"*Acchha, ap Samar ho?*"

"*Haan, ji.*"

"*Aapka saamaan ready hai,* sir. I'll just match it from the list once," the shopkeeper said.

"Sure."

Just as I turned away to look at the place while the shopkeeper got me my stuff, I heard a voice call my name me.

"Hey, Samar!" Navya shouted to get my attention.

"Oh, hi," I turned towards her and said.

"Lost?"

"Not this time. I know where I am!"

"Shit! I thought I would get to show you the way," she said faking a sad expression.

"I have absolutely no idea which corner of the world I am in. Could you please help me, kind lady?" I asked super-seriously.

She laughed at my expression and shook her head. "Drama. Anyway, what are you doing here?"

"Just getting stuff for Joseph."

"Oh, okay. Need help?"

"Sure. You can carry all these bags for me," I said and motioned to the three heavy bags lying at the store's counter.

"Excuse me? Do I know you?" she frowned.

I laughed, paid the shopkeeper, picked up the bags and started to walk. "Let's go."

"I can hold one of them if you want," Navya offered.

"Generous of you, but no thanks. I will manage."

"Whatever suits you. Anyway, so, what are you doing after this?"

"I don't know. Whatever Joseph asks me to, I guess," I said.

"Oh. So you don't have time…"

"For?"

"I was wondering… No. Nothing," she said and shut up.

"What? Tell me!"

"Umm… I am kind of a big Hanuman fan. And it's a Tuesday. I thought that if you had time…"

"You want me to visit a temple with you?" I asked.

"Yes. But I understand if you are busy. You need to take care of work too…"

"Do you know of any temple nearby?"

"Yes. There is this—" she started to say but I cut her off.

"How much time would it take us to get there and back?"

"Twenty minutes. Half an hour, tops."

"Cool then. I would tell Joseph I would not be available for an hour," I said.

"But you don't have to! I understand if you have work to take care of."

"I know. But my work does not start this early anyway. I am sure it would be okay."

"Okay," she said casually, but her smile said a lot more. She was genuinely happy that I wanted to go with her. She was very easy to please. Give her the small things in life and she would be happy.

And I felt like I was born to make her happy. I could never deny her anything, except my love. That was something Kanika took with her. She had marked me as hers permanently, even though I no longer had her in return. I did not feel like I even had the ability to fall in love again. And so, I felt bad for myself. I sometimes pitied the condition I was in. I felt even worse for Navya.

When Navya was done with her prayers, we started walking back.

"You don't seem very religious," Navya said, looking at me.

"Yeah. I'm not."

"Can I ask why?"

"Well, because I believe that God wants us to be atheists," I replied.

"What do you mean?"

"I mean if I was God, I would really want you to be an atheist."

"And you say that because...?" she asked.

"Because atheists are people who really take things in their hands instead of praying to God for everything."

"Why did I even bother to argue," Navya said, and smiled at me.

And seeing her smile, I suddenly remembered again – I loved to see her smile.

Over the next few weeks, Navya and I came really close. We went on evening walks on the beach, bare foot, talking randomly. I liked her even more when she was in her random-mode. I was getting used to it. You could never guess what she was going to say next. Her moods changed very quickly and so did the tone of her voice. I liked all that.

We went to the temple on Tuesdays. It was as if going there was an unspoken ritual between us. Every Tuesday, as soon as I woke up and took a shower, I would find Navya waiting for me outside. And wordlessly, we would start walking towards the temple. We talked all through the way, but never about where we were going and why.

We drank together every now and then, got sloshed and sometimes caused havoc around the place. Everything with Navya was fun. And we talked for hours and hours. Amazingly, I somehow managed to keep her off one closed chapter of my life – Kanika. And she never asked much about her either. She began to literally occupy every minute that I was not working.

If someone saw us together, he would be very sure that we were madly in love with each other. That is how we looked from a distance. We were always together, always happy, and didn't care about the rest of the world. We looked very love-soaked.

But we were not. At least I was not. She definitely was. Sometimes she used to look at me strangely. She used to have a serious expression on her face and she said nothing, but the look in her eyes said it all. She was in love with me. My bare foot evening walk with her on the beach became the only thing I looked forward to, when I got up every afternoon; the only thing I thought of was the evening walk with her.

And when I went to sleep, I felt good about life. I knew this feeling, of having someone to talk to. It was the first time I was having a friend apart from Roy. And I loved every minute I spent with her.

That afternoon, when I went to sleep, I compared my friendship with Navya with what I had with Roy. I missed the good times I had spent with Roy. But why did he have to do that? There were half a billion other girls in the country. Why? Why? Why?

"Hey, handsome," Navya said to me, as she walked up to me one evening.

I looked back to check who she was talking to. Apparently, that was addressed to me.

She smiled. "Why are you so uncomfortable with compliments?"

"Because I was bullied a lot as a kid for my looks."

She laughed out loud on hearing that. She must have pictured a nasty bunch of guys pulling my curly hair.

"Aw, that's sweet. But I don't think they would bully you now, you giant," she said poking fun at my six foot plus something frame.

"Thanks," I said, repeating myself. Navya kept looking at me. As if she was studying my embarrassed behaviour. She kept quiet for a second as if she was thinking what to say next.

"Why do you hold back so much?" she finally asked.

"What do you mean?"

"I mean why are you so reserved to anything pleasant in life?"

"I am a very fun loving person," I defended myself.

"Reading newspapers is not fun."

"I don't read the newspapers."

"You get what I mean," she said.

I did get what she meant. There was a brief silence. Navya was great at arguing. It wasn't always easy thinking of answers to the questions that she threw at me. She would say things that would totally catch you off-guard and you would not be able to find a reply to prove otherwise. How can she be so right about things?

"I want to know more about you, Samar," she said.

"There is nothing to know."

"Why are you here?"

"Because I don't like it back in Delhi," I replied shortly. That was one conversation I did not want to have.

"Shut up. There's more to it. I want to know."

"I don't want to talk about it."

"I don't have much time in Goa. Any evening could be our last one together," she said sadly.

"What do you mean?"

"I mean my dad would find out I am not in Bhopal anytime."

"Then what will he do?" I asked.

"He will hunt me down and reach WoodStock Village within hours."

"Oh okay. And what after that? Will we ever talk after you leave?"

"No," she said.

"No?"

"No."

"And how do you say that with so much confidence?" I asked.

"Because I *am* confident about it. There is no way we will talk again."

"Okay."

"What *okay?* I am telling you that I might leave Goa any day now, to never come back. And that once I leave here, I would not be in touch with you. That we would never see each other, never hear from each other... We would have no idea how the other is doing... We would have absolutely no contacts from... *tomorrow*, maybe. And that is your only reaction? *"Okay?"* Is it *okay* with you?" she was shouting. People were looking at us, trying to figure out what was happening.

"Navya... I did not mean—"

"Then what did you fucking mean, Samar? You are *okay* if I suddenly disappear? If I suddenly leave... and never come back? If I just *go?* Forever? *Would it not affect you if I am fucking dead?*"

I did not know how to respond to that. I had never seen Navya like that. She had always come across as someone who did not care too much about anything. And yes, I knew she was attached to me, but I did not know the extent to which she was so. I did not intend to hurt her in any way. But it turned out that I had been doing exactly that.

I opened my mouth to say something but I could think of nothing that would control the damage. I knew I would never love her the way I loved Kanika. So I did not want to say anything to Navya that would give her false hopes.

She had to get over me.

"You're special, Navya," was all I could say. And I said it so meekly that I was sure she did not even hear me. Until I heard her say something, equally softly.

"But you do not love me."

"Yes, I do not love you."

"And you never will," she said. It was a statement.

I nodded wordlessly. It hurt me to see her hurt like that. Especially knowing that I was the reason behind all her pain. But there was nothing I could do. Kanika had ruined me for everyone else.

We sat there silently for a while. She seemed lost in thoughts, and I was sure those thoughts were not pleasant ones. She was looking exceptionally sad that day, after the conversation we had.

I wanted to kick myself for doing that to her. I broke the promise I had made to myself once. *I promised myself that for the rest of my life, I will take great care of this girl, no matter where I am. This girl was special.*

"Tell me why you are here, Samar Garg," she whispered.

And I had to succumb. I had no reason to not to tell her. And that was the only way to make her understand how much Kanika meant to me and why I could not fall in love with anyone else. So, I told her everything.

Okay. To be honest, I did not tell her everything. Just the end. She already knew I had a girlfriend I was deeply in love with. So I did not go into details about that. Instead, I went into details about how it ended. About how I saw her kiss my best friend and how it made me feel. And so, she understood why I ran to Goa. I had sheen of tears in my eyes by the time my story ended.

I knew what that meant. That meant that no matter how successful I am in keeping thoughts of Kanika away, she was the one I would always love. I could never hate her. Even after what she did to me…

"I respect you even more now, Samar," Navya said, after she heard everything I told her.

"Respect?"

"Yeah. I mean after all that has happened, you have still built this wall around you. You still do not let any other girl in…"

"It is not deliberate. It is something which has just happened," I said.

"You are a very nice person, Samar."

"Hmm."

"I promise I wouldn't make it any tougher for you," she said and gave me her signature blank look, impervious to any interpretation.

"What do you mean?"

"You will see tomorrow morning," she said, as she typed a message on her phone and sent it.

"Have you told your *goonda* friends to beat me up?"

She looked at me blankly. Nobody could ever look at her and tell what was going through her head. I had no idea how she did it. It was as if, at the age of nineteen, she knew everything there was to know about people. As if nothing surprised her. As if she was expecting whatever was happening.

"You must have really loved her?" she asked.

I stayed quiet. I didn't want to talk about Kanika. Talking about her made me miss her, which was something I really wasn't interested in.

"Was she beautiful?" she asked next.

"Very."

"See. You totally loved her."

"What?" I asked. This was one of those things she said that struck the bull's-eye and left me wondering *how-the-hell-does-she-know?*

"You should have heard your 'very'."

"Hmmm."

"So, who confessed the love first?" she asked.

"You think I am going to tell you?"

"Yes," Navya said and stared at me, with a smile. I know people smile all the time. A lot of time we don't even notice that someone is smiling. But when Navya smiles, people stop their cars and watch. I was sure she could make Prime Ministers change their national policies with a smile. I was just a homeless hotel employee. I was disarmed.

"I did," I said, unwillingly.

"How?"

I sighed. I could see she was not going to give up easily.

"Well, we were in Andaman and Nicobar islands at that time. I took her to a lonely island where the two of us were the only people present. Except the jazz band that I had arranged. So on the lonely beach, in the background of the jazz music, I had arranged a table and a chair and some Mexican food. At the right moment, I got down on my knee and confessed every thought of her that crossed my mind."

I looked at Navya. Same trademark blank look.

"It went on for quite a while," I said. "I started from what I had thought when I saw her for the first time. And I ended with that moment there, how she looked."

"I know you too well to believe that. I think you must have done something extravagant. But not *this* for sure."

"Yeah. It was pretty stylish. But it seems so juvenile now," I said.

"Because she cheated on you?"

"Not just that. It was genuinely kiddish."

"What did you do?" she asked.

I then told her what I did for her and felt quite stupid doing so.

"You are more romantic than I thought," she said.

"As I said, it all sounds so juvenile now."

Navya looked at me. But this time it wasn't with blank eyes. I saw curiosity in her eyes. It was as if she was trying to figure me out.

"Samar... you don't seem the type."

"What type?"

"The *running away* type, I mean. You don't seem like someone who would do that," she said. And added softly, "You must be a good guy to have in one's life" she added.

I smiled and pressed my lips. And then, she suddenly turned all quiet. She said nothing, just kept looking at me. This went on for two whole minutes and I realised she had no intention of looking away. It was getting weird.

"You know you are creeping me out, don't you?" I said and laughed a dry laugh.

She said nothing, but a sad smile crept to her face. The look in her eyes would have melted anyone on the planet. No one would ever want to deny anything to her. She was just way too sweet to keep anything from. And at that moment, she looked sad. That is the only way to describe it. That is the only word. *Sad*.

I felt like giving her a big hug, and telling her that everything will be alright. I felt like saying something funny, to make her laugh. I felt like crying.

Instead, I asked, "Navya, why are you looking at me like that?"

I expected her to say something like, "What? So now I can't even look?" but she didn't. She said something that left me speechless. I think the slight wetness in her eyes also contributed to my sudden loss of ability to speak.

Her voice was a whisper as she said, "Sometimes, you just look at things you know you can never have..."

21
When the going gets tough

Next day, Navya came to wake me up from sleep and join her for a walk. There was something almost desperate in her way. I felt like she was hiding something… as if something bad was going to happen. I understood nothing of it. And I did not ask her anything about it either. I was scared to ask. I did not want the answer.

We walked on the beach, silently for a while. The sun was about to set and the scene was pretty. The reddish sky reflected on the water and gave it its colour. Things were beautiful around me.

Especially Navya. Her hair, which was usually tied carelessly behind, was let loose that evening. And it was flying behind her with the wind. But what I liked best was – when we turned around and the wind started to blow from the opposite side, her hair was a mess. A pretty mess. I watched her as she struggled to manage it and tuck the strands behind her ears. And failed miserably.

Next, her skirt started to fly too. Before I could see much, she gave up on her hair and tried feverishly to keep her skirt in place. She looked pissed. That only made her look cuter.

"Never wear a skirt to a beach," she muttered under her breath.

"Sure. I promise I won't," I replied.

"What?"

"No. Nothing."

We kept walking and the wind let Navya off the hook after a bit of teasing. She finally stopped struggling with her hair and skirt. Darn. I was having fun.

But she was in one of her *I'm-in-a-different-world* modes. I waited for it. I knew she was going to say something heavy.

There was something about my conversations with Navya. It was as if we were talking at a higher level. As if we were both ahead of our ages and both of us knew where the other was coming from. When we talked side by side, there was never anything awkward about the silence. And yet, her eyes always remained blank.

"What is wrong with me?" she asked me after some time.

"What is wrong with you?"

"You know what I mean, Samar. And you know what is wrong with me. Tell me what it is."

"There is nothing wrong with you," I said.

"You are not helping me by not telling me."

"I just don't think I know you," I said.

"Because... you don't know me."

"I really want to know what made you what you are," I said.

"What do you mean?"

"You know what I mean."

"What do you want to know?" she sighed.

"That what made you who you are."

"My uncle."

"How?" I prodded.

"He abused me when I was a kid. He used to stare at me all the time when I was fourteen. I never knew why it was so weird. And then, one day, when I was alone in the house, he locked the door. He looked at me like no one ever had. I felt as if he would tear me apart and eat me."

Fuck. So this was the real Navya. I could see the seething hatred in her eyes.

"He held my hands and forced me to go naked. When I refused, he beat me up."

She was breathing heavy by then. It was like telling the story itself was costing her too much effort. She had a pained expression on her face. And her eyes were not blank. They were expressing the loathe she felt for her uncle. And they always displayed a gamut of other emotions. Disgust. Fear. Fury.

I did not know what to say next. I felt pure anger towards that bastard. If he had been in front of me, I would have torn him apart. I wanted to take Navya's revenge from him. I could not bear the thought of anyone hurting her. And the way that man did...

"How does it feel now?" I asked, controlling my own emotions and concentrating on making Navya feel better.

"How do you think it feels? What a stupid question."

"I mean... does it still wake you up at night? Or does it barely cross your mind?"

"I think of it several times a day. Every day. It never leaves me. It's always somewhere at the back of my head. Every time I take a shower..." she trailed away.

I digested the information. "What happens when you see your uncle?"

"I have never seen him again after that."

"How did you manage to do that?"

"I make sure I am not around whenever he is expected home," she said.

"Hmm."

Suddenly, it changed the way I saw Navya. Until that moment, I had thought she was a rich kid, spoilt by too much love by her parents. But she was something else. I felt sympathy for her. But the best I could do was to keep my hand over hers, look at her and give a reassuring look, saying all was going to be okay from here on. She smiled.

"You really like me, don't you?" I asked.

She paused for a second, holding my gaze. And then she said it. "I am crazy about you, Samar."

"Can I know why?"

"You are an amazing person. You have changed the way I look at myself," she said.

"What do you mean?"

"I mean before I met you, I felt I was a guy with boobs. No, seriously. I had no traits of a girl and I didn't even emote like them. I hated dressing up or putting on makeup."

"So what has changed now?"

"Everything! Every-*fucking*-thing. You have changed everything. You make me want to dress up. You make me smile at myself silently. You make me feel like a girl. All those emotions I had never imagined are coming to me. You are doing that to me, Samar."

"I didn't mean to," I said.

She smiled. And then she mentioned it too. "See. You have even started making me smile!"

The next evening, I woke up and carried out my daily routine. As I was brushing my teeth, it struck me. Navya had said the previous evening that I was going to find out what she meant when she said that she was going to make it easier for me.

I went out and looked around. There were more than a few people standing in the open area. Something was happening. I hoped it was not because of her.

I went closer to the crowd to see what was happening. I saw a man pulling Navya by her arm. I saw his face and it was more than clear that he was Navya's father. The resemblance was unmistakable.

He was shouting at the top of his voice. And most people living in WoodStock Village had gathered, watching. It was a rare sight for them. For the foreigners, it must have been unprecedented.

Navya's father was shouting.

"How dare you just run away from home? On top of that, you had the guts to message me your address!" he shouted.

A part of the crowd seemed to be enjoying it. Another part was just bemused as to what was happening.

Meanwhile, her father continued the shouting. "Wait till we reach home. Your mother can't stop crying."

For me, throughout all this, what was most striking was Navya's expression. Her signature blank look was dropped. There was, in fact, a weak side of Navya. Her stoic-self gave way to a regular nineteen year old girl. And I saw her come close to tears. As her father held her hand and half threw her into the cab, she looked at me in the eye.

Her eyes were saying only one thing. *Why Samar, why? Why can't we be together?*

As the car sped away, I felt engulfed in emptiness. What was worse was that I didn't have any contact details of her. I didn't even have her mobile number. All I knew was that she was from Indore. And she did not have my contact number. We had broken all ties.

She disappeared from my life. Forever.

Once Navya left, the crowd which had gathered felt a little weird. But then, one after the other, everyone went back to their rooms. But I kept standing there. It was all too sudden for me to digest.

I knew the look on Navya's face the previous evening meant something was going to happen, but I had not guessed it was something of this magnitude. She left and left me with a void in my heart.

That look on her face pierced something deep inside me. I had not expected that Navya's leaving will hit me so hard. I felt strength getting drained out of my body. I somehow stumbled to my place in the village. I reached the rug sack where I used to sleep. I looked at the beach in front. Suddenly, it all seemed meaningless. I picked my rug, my bedding and left the place. And started walking towards nothing in particular. I just wanted to be away from the place which smelled of Navya, all over.

I went to the beach, a little further from WoodStock and

spread the rug on the sand and lied down on it. And kept lying there till indefinite time.

When I opened my eyes again, it had gotten pretty dark. My head was still heavy from everything that happened. Navya. I will never see her again. She was gone. She was over, as far as my life was concerned.

Why didn't I push her for her phone number?

Why couldn't I just ask her address, her email ID, anything at all?

Or was it best that she had gone. Maybe, some chapters should end in life, so that they remain a splendid memory forever.

With a hangover of random thoughts, I made my way back for WoodStock. I looked at the village and was thinking of only one thing. I had nothing to look forward to in that place, as if all the positivity had been sucked out of it.

I had nothing left to do. Apart from work, she was what occupied all my time. Just then, a thought came to me. *Work.* That was the only thing that could distract me. I needed to be occupied to stay sane. I caught on with Joseph. I had to find a brand new clutter for my head and Joseph was the only person who could have given me that.

Joseph was a little startled on seeing me.

"Samar? Where were you? We thought you went back to Delhi!"

"I just needed some time by myself."

"Okay. So tell me, what's up?" he asked.

"Joseph, I was thinking, the time has come that you went home for Christmas."

"What? Why would I go home for Christmas?"

"You said you always wanted to celebrate Christmas with your family. And I think this is a good time to fulfil your wish," I said.

"And who is going to run WoodStock behind me? Christmas is a big day for us."

"How big?"

"It is pretty big. We expect a turnout of almost a hundred and fifty people every year," he said.

"We will manage, Joseph. This is a vacation you really need."

"Are you kidding me? This place will come crashing down the moment I let it out of my sight."

"You are not as important as you think," I said, repeating what he had said to me once.

"This place is not as capable as you think."

"It is. And you know that. Give it a chance."

"Look at you... Twenty one years of age and wants to run everything," he said, still not caving in.

"I know everything there is to know about this place. You have groomed me that way. I know how *everything* here works."

"I have ensured you know everything there is to know in this place. But to handle it all without me..."

Joseph was not giving up and I knew it was a lost battle if I tried to convince him. *More pressure.* I signalled Thimappa to join in the discussion. He walked in, trying to understand what was happening.

"I was telling Joseph that he should celebrate this Christmas with his family in Kerala, leaving WoodStock to us."

Thimappa figured out everything in a second. He understood that I wanted to run this place in our way when Joseph was gone, like we had talked about earlier.

"Awesome idea. I have always wanted Joseph to be with his family for Christmas," Thimappa joined in.

Joseph paused for a second. And the pause was my lead. I knew I had got him thinking. Even though he was turning down the idea fervently. I could see that all he needed was some convincing.

"Samar, when I was your age, I was a waiter in a small shack in Kerala," Joseph said.

"Even I am a waiter two nights every week," I said.

"But I have no reason to believe you will not be able to run this place." Joseph said and fell silent. He must have been carrying out a mental check of all the responsibilities at WoodStock and analysing whether I was capable of managing them all or not.

And then, he nodded.

"Okay, Kerala it is then, this Christmas," he said.

Thimappa and I rejoiced and high fived.

"But there is one condition," Joseph added. "In the next one week before I leave, you will have to convince me that you are capable of running this place."

"Done!" Thimappa and I said in chorus.

That is exactly what I loved about my life at WoodStock Village.

Firstly, life seemed to keep throwing challenges one after the other. And these were challenges no one had ever thought of in Delhi. Staying in Delhi might have taught me every theorem ever written in every book, but it would have never given me the street smartness that only Goa offered.

Secondly, when I stood in the open area of the Village and looked all around, no two people ever seemed the same. I mean – you looked at their faces and you knew that everybody came from a completely different world altogether. On one side there was Joseph, a Keral-ite living in Goa. Then there was Thimappa. And then there were the guests, from twelve different countries, wailing their time in Goa for one reason or the other. There was no pattern in their life's story. Each was unique.

Thirdly, things kept happening in WoodStock Village. One moment you are having one of the best conversations of your life with a girl from Indore. The next moment you are sleeping. The next moment you wake up to her being reprimanded and dragged home by her dad. The next moment you are gearing up for the most challenging work task of your life – convincing Joseph that you are good enough.

I felt stimulated. I felt the depression of Navya's departure lighten up on me. But before I got time to wallow in grief, I had found a way to dodge the pain. There was no other way. I could not keep thinking about Navya without hurting. If I thought of her all the time, like I used to, I was sure I would not be able to bear it. The pain would be too much.

In the time we had spent together in Goa, I had become used to her presence. She was a part of my world there. A big part. I had created a new world for myself, running to Goa and living there. And Navya was an indispensible part of it. With her gone, I did not even want to think about how I would manage to survive each day...

And that's why I had found myself a distraction. More responsibility of the shack would mean lesser free time. Which meant – lesser haunting thoughts. And so, I eventually started to look forward to the next week.

Next day, I cleaned up, changed to my work clothes and went to look for Thimappa. We would have to manage the situation together behind Joseph.

We went up to him and flashed our broadest smiles. We were ready to be assigned tasks.

"Hi Joseph," I said.

Joseph looked at us. He saw our smile and seemed to like it. We were radiating confidence. This was one thing we really wanted to do. And we were willing to work hard to make it work. Although I had decided to use it just as a distraction, eventually I started looking forward to it for other reasons. For Joseph – he would get to celebrate Christmas with his family. For Thimappa – he would get to organize the Christmas bash himself. Plus, of course – I would get something that would keep me occupied at most times.

"So both of you are absolutely sure that you can manage this?" Joseph asked.

We smiled.

"See Thimappa, until now, you have always been looking

after the kitchen. If you want to do this, you will have to manage other things too. Like – housekeeping, getting vegetables, God knows what not."

"It is not as tough as you make it sound," Thimappa replied. Joseph liked his confidence.

"And you, Samar, until now, you spend your night working on one thing. If you do this, you would have to spend hours working on everything every night."

I nodded.

And hence began the most hectic week of my life. Joseph delegated work between both of us and told us what to do if something goes wrong. I hardly slept for the next few days. If times had been hectic till now, the next one week was crazy. Every minute of every day, Joseph was downloading information on us. We kept soaking in as much of it as we could. I used to be tired even when I woke up. We were testing our own breaking strength. But on the seventh day, you should have seen the smile on Joseph's face. He looked like a Prisoner of War who was being freed after years of incarceration. He was finally spending his Christmas with his family.

And then came his time to leave. He looked at me with kind eyes, as if I was his own son. He hugged me and Thimappa before leaving and left WoodStock Village like a very satisfied man. That was the second bye I said on that doorstep, even though it was a temporary one. But it was a huge responsibility on my shoulders.

I turned around and looked at all the employees of WoodStock Village. They were all going to look up at me for instructions. I looked at Thimappa. He looked a little intimidated.

This was the real thing now. No turning back. Nobody to take advice from. Nobody to guide us through this. We were just relying on whatever we had learnt.

22

The Big Bash

"So how many people come for the Christmas party?" I asked Thimappa. We were in Joseph's room. It was time the two of us sat together and discussed how we were doing it.

"We expect at least one hundred people to come. But my guess would be around a hundred and fifty people."

"We are going to target two hundred and fifty people."

Thimappa looked at me. He must have seen ambition in my eyes. "But how will you make more people come in? Do you want decrease the alcohol prices?" he asked.

"Joseph will kill us if he comes to know of that. Also, I don't think many people care about the price when they are partying in Goa."

"Then what do you have in mind?"

"We could put up posters all around," I suggested.

"Nobody reads posters in Goa. No one would notice."

"Still, it's pretty cheap. Even if ten people turn up because of them, it will be worth it," I said.

"Where will we get them printed?" Thimappa asked.

"We will just take print outs at a cyber café. That should be enough."

"And you think people will come in on reading those print outs?"

"Yes," I said with great conviction.

I went to the cyber café nearby and scribbled some lines on Microsoft Word and gave the print command. But nothing happened. I talked to the café owner and he told me that the printer was not working. So I decided to hand write one poster and photocopy it. I knew Thimappa would freak out if he saw a handwritten poster. But still, I was sure it was better than nothing.

I made fifty photocopies of the page. I put the copies on the most prominent locations on the beaches of Goa. And kept the original copy with myself. I have it even today. And there is no way I can resist sharing it here.

ONE PARTY YOUR FRIENDS DIDN'T TELL YOU ABOUT!

WELCOME TO THE MOST EXCLUSIVE PARTY IN GOA.

A PARTY IN THE MIDDLE OF A LESSER KNOWN BEACH!

THE BIGGEST CHRISTMAS PARTY!

IF YOU CAN FIND IT, YOU WOULD NEVER WANT TO LEAVE.

WOODSTOCK VILLAGE, ARAMBOL.

OR CALL +91 9898989898

People look for exclusivity. The words 'exclusive' and 'never' want to leave was sure to send some exciting vibes. I was sure that line would pique some interest in the people who read it. Or that is what I hoped for.

Thimappa and I paid attention to every detail of every square inch of WoodStock. I made sure every inch was clean. Thimappa made sure every dish had the exact right amount of salt and other condiments. We procured the best vegetables available in the market. And I arranged enough alcohol for two hundred and fifty people. Thimappa wasn't very supportive of the big investment, but I was sure the poster would work. I don't remember praying harder than I did that day.

On the afternoon of the twenty fourth December, I had only three hours to sleep. I could not sleep out of the excitement I felt about the next day. And nervousness, of course. We had worked hard for the bash, and I prayed for nothing to go wrong. It was going to be the big evening. It was the Christmas eve, the night when everybody from everywhere in the world was going to swarm to Goa and jump onto the best party they could find.

I had put up posters of the big party all around. Each and every beach in the city had some mention of our Christmas party. And I was sure that they would help us. Even if they fetched just a handful of customers, it would be worth it.

There was lots of work still to be done. First of all, I had to upscale my daily activities. If I made ten kilos of pasta every day, that day I had to make twenty. And then, there were things I had to do which I didn't do normally. Like Christmas decoration, mid night cake etc. It was not exactly hard work, but taken together, it certainly was a lot of work. But amazingly, it did not dampen my mood. I was actually looking forward to working. And that was not only because of the fact that it would keep my mind off Kanika… and Navya. Though that was one of the reasons too.

I wanted the party to be a big hit. For Thimappa, who had wanted it for such a long time. For Joseph, who had left the place to us, trusting us to take good care of things. For myself, to keep me busy, and to prove everyone and myself that I was capable enough.

At four in the afternoon, I called everybody who worked for WoodStock to the lawn.

"Okay, everyone. Tonight is the night. We have all worked

very hard for this and I do not want anything to go wrong," I said. "We all know what we have to do now. And it's time to get started. Ask each and every question you want to right now, but I want all of you to be absolutely clear about what you have to do."

I knew I was acting bossy. It wasn't my natural self to act like that. But then, it was the need of that hour. I was serious about it and people could see that. And it was my job to make sure that everyone else took it seriously too. I mentally ran a check of whether everyone knew their job or not. I believed they did. As long as everyone did his assigned piece of work efficiently, things would be fine. And then, I got down to my own job. I had made a list of all jobs which were to be done. So I started checking one thing after the other.

At eight o'clock, I called all my boys to the lawn and gave them a final set of instructions. I looked at their faces. The entertainment guys had been working for a long time and some of them were almost double my age. And yet, they were listening intently. I felt good about myself. I had managed to command respect from them, purely because I had worked hard.

People started coming in at around nine in the evening. I made a cross and hoped for the best.

As I kept running from one corner to another, I kept a count of the number of people in the villa. A part of me wanted more and more people to come. But the other part of me knew that we weren't really prepared for too many people.

By ten thirty, there were already a hundred people in the place. I knew it was going to be an adventurous evening.

As I ran into the kitchen, I realized that Thimappa had been looking for me.

"Where the fuck were you?" he shouted at me.

"I was taking care of the bar. Why? What happened?"

"And why the fuck do you not carry a fucking phone?"

"Will you just tell me what happened?" I asked.

"By the looks of things, I think we can have a shortage of food later…"

There were two parts of WoodStock that night. One part was partying, oblivious to anything happening behind the scenes in that area. Another part was running around, making sure that the place doesn't fall apart.

Every single employee of WoodStock was looking for me. There was not a moment when I wasn't tackling one problem or the other. Housekeeping, food, fights, I handled them all.

At twelve, there was a grand toast. For me, it was a momentary breather, so that I could get my senses back in place.

Throughout all this, I had only one major concern. As long as these people had beer in their mugs, they could live with an unclean patch on their table or a little extra salt in their food. And that's how things ran smoothly for the initial part of the night. But soon, we were close to running out of alcohol. There was not enough of it to last the night. And those people looked rowdy. They could damage more than what I could have afforded. They didn't walk all their way through rocky roads to a party that didn't have alcohol.

As I stood in a corner, I tried to count the number of people there. My guess was – two hundred and eighty. Which meant we would run out of alcohol by three. It was a terrible news for me.

What Joseph used to say suddenly crossed my mind. "I invite only as many people as I can serve." I finally saw sense in his words.

If those people ran out of alcohol, WoodStock would forever be that creepy place where they once went and had a terrible time. I raked my brain to think of a solution. But nothing came to my mind.

The crowd was close to stampede level. The logistics of the place began to fall apart. Nobody out of those people would ever come back. I could not let that happen. I could not let Joseph down like that. I had promised him that I would take care of WoodStock Village in his absence. Moreover, it was not just Joseph and the place which would suffer. Thimappa would also be affected. So would be my self-worth.

I ran to the kitchen and told Thimappa that we were going to run out of alcohol. I told him everything and my worst fear came true. Thimappa was as clueless as I was.

"Now what are we going to do?" I asked him.

"I don't know! You tell me what we are going to do!" he said.

"Joseph is going to kill us."

"Forget Joseph, I'm going to kill you!" Thimappa shouted.

I ran out of the kitchen and looked at the happy people. I had a scary vision of how the same place would look if we ran out of alcohol.

I thought hard, to remember if in the time I had spent in Goa, I had heard of a place that had a big enough supply of alcohol in the middle of the night. At first, I drew a blank. And then it struck me. *Inspector Neelesh Mesta*, the Goan who always stocked alcohol. I remembered Joseph having mentioned something about it.

I couldn't think of a reason for him to help me. I had met him once to get a friend released of jail and he had once found me sleeping on a beach, penniless, jobless. But for lack of my options, I ran to him anyway. I reached the police station and prayed Neelesh Mesta would be there. He was. It was *his* police station, after all, as he once said.

I had never expected I would be so happy to see him. He was sitting on his chair, half sleeping and half awake. And to my intense surprise, when he spotted me, he seemed genuinely happy.

"Now what, bastard?" Neelesh asked, half-smiling.

"Hi Neelesh," I said, smiling.

"I am sure you need a huge favour from me."

It wasn't that tough to guess after seeing how embarrassed I looked. I said, "Actually, I am running WoodStock Village now—"

"How much alcohol do you want?" Neelesh cut me in between. It seemed like many shack owners used to go to him for alcohol.

"Twenty litres of whisky and one hundred and fifty litres of beer," I said. "At least."

"Ram Prasad, give him whatever he asks. And give him five percent discount too."

"Thank you, sir," I said.

Getting the alcohol turned out to be a lucky break. I thanked him for his support and made my way back in the vehicle carrying the liquor. When I got back to WoodStock Village, Thimappa could not believe what I had done. He had invested a lifetime on the streets of Goa. But fetching alcohol on the Christmas eve was something unprecedented even for him.

That was what living in Goa was all about. You never knew what you will be doing today. You did not know who you would meet today. You had no idea what kind of problem will face you. I was not complaining. In fact, I loved every minute of it.

I loved the unpredictability of my life.

23

Resisting the Temptation

"Where is my beer?" one man shouted at the bar counter at WoodStock.

"Sir, we have run out of it," the bartender responded.

"What do you mean *run out of it*? It is not even two!"

"Sir, we are trying get more. Just give us thirty minutes," the bartender said.

"In half an hour, I would be fucking out of this shit-hole. You can shove your bottle of beer up your ass by then," the man said.

"Sir, please try to understand. We are trying our best to—" the bartender tried to plead, but the customer cut him off.

"Shut up, you dumb-fuck! If you can't run this place, why open it?" he shouted. He then held his girlfriend's hand and started to walkout of WoodStock.

Same thing followed with a few more people. That was when I came out from the kitchen, after having unloaded the fresh stacks of alcohol. I saw quite a few people leaving. I realized I had to take a corrective action quickly. The temper of the crowd was rising pretty fast. By the time the bartender would start serving the alcohol, irreversible damage would have happened. I rushed to the stage, where the drummers were playing and asked for a mike. I asked him to turn down the volume of the music and started making an announcement. I held the mike and faced the crowd.

"Merry Christmas everyone!" I shouted. The crowd shouted

back. As expected, their tone was not merry. It was angry. But at least I had their attention. I continued, "I know we have had some problems with alcohol tonight but it is not my mistake. You guys seem to love alcohol a little too much!"

There was a roar from the crowd, appreciating themselves.

"Anyway, the good news is that things are in place now. And you know what? Each and every one of you gets a free pint of beer for bearing with us!" I said and the crowd erupted. I thought I had managed the crowd by saying that. In five minutes, the beer had reached the bartender.

The crowd seemed to love the party, as I looked on like a satisfied man. I mentally calculated the cost of free beer I had given away and I knew Joseph wouldn't kill me for that. We were still earning a lot from the food people were hogging once they were drunk. I went to check how things were going in the kitchen. There was a lot of bustle around the place. Thimappa was instructing some assistant to do something when I approached him.

"All is okay?" I asked.

"Yes. We will have enough food in twenty minutes," he said with a smile.

"Really? That quick? But how?" I asked. I was amazed. I had not expected the food issue to be sorted at all, let alone so soon!

"Don't you worry about that. I have been in this place for quite some time now. I know how to handle this," Thimappa said, rather proudly.

I left the kitchen with a wide smile on my face. I took a sigh of relief. The whole gig turned out to be okay. In fact, it was all better than what I had expected. Joseph would be happy, I was sure. I took a place in a corner and watched as people danced happily to the beats that the drummers played. They were drunk. Their bellies were full. They were happy. It was Christmas and it looked so. At certain moments, I wanted to get sloshed too, but then I had a job at hand.

The party was a hit. No major brawls. People ignored the slight shortage of food because of alcohol. They discovered a place they had never heard of before, and partied in a completely new ambience. As the relief swept over, I could not help but think of Navya. I wondered how she would have reacted had she known what we did that night. Would she have been as proud as I thought she would have been?

Moreover, I wished that she was there not just to see me accomplish what I had, but also to spend Christmas Eve with me. The void she left behind when she left was still very much there. I had no friends there to share good times with. I missed her.

The happiness seemed rather empty without her. And then it struck me. Navya had taken over my thoughts completely. It had been a while since I had thought of Kanika. That was definitely good news, simply because missing Navya was a sweet pain. But Kanika was a bitter pain, which I wouldn't want anyone to have.

Life moves on.

The last guest left at eight in the morning, while many of them took rooms at WoodStock and crashed there itself. For the first time since it was opened, WoodStock was completely occupied. Thimappa and I hadn't taken a breath all evening, night and morning.

"Merry Christmas," Thimappa said, as the two of us sat on two lonely chairs kept in the middle of all the junk lying all around.

"Happy Christmas, Thimappa," I replied.

"It was a good party."

"Good? It was a fucking AWESOME party," I said.

"So this is where the happy part ends," Thimappa said, seeing the ominous task ahead of us.

"Thimappa?"

"Yes?"

"Why do we have to clean up the place before going to sleep every day?" I asked.

"Because if we don't, the place will stink a little by the time we wake up."

"But once we would clean it, it would stop stinking, right?"

"Yeah," he said and looked at me uncertainly, as if wondering what I was up to.

"Then why not clean the place in the evening, when we wake up?"

Thimappa thought for a second. "But—"

"Blah, it is not important enough," I cut him in between.

Thimappa smiled, conceding. "But I am not sleepy yet," he said.

"Who said we are going to sleep?"

"Then what will we do?"

"We are a bunch of twenty boys. And we have sixty bottles of beer with us," I said.

Thimappa's smile knew no bounds. We called everyone who worked at WoodStock and passed a bottle to everyone.

That had never happened before at WoodStock. I finished a bottle faster than I normally used to. Beer and abuses were flowing in the air. The music also started in a while, with the drummers and guitarists happily drunk. All the boys took to the floor. We didn't care for the guests who were staying at WoodStock and had just gone to sleep after partying all night. We were soaked in our own euphoria.

I moved onto my second bottle, and finished it faster than I could usually have managed. I hadn't slept well for almost two weeks. And I had worked almost every waking hour. My body was crying for rest. My head was whizzing because of all those combined effects. I could have fallen on the ground in nausea. I had no clue what was happening around me. On top of it all, the sun was shining on my head. The December sun is no less relentless in Goa. It could make your head spin worse than many things.

"Here, have some tequila too," Thimappa said, and handed me a bottle of half-finished Tequila.

I took the bottle, pressed it against my lips and finished it.

If my head had been whizzing till then, it went into a frenzy after that. The tequila showed its effects. I felt energy being sapped out of my body. My legs started to get loose. We kept dancing to the loud music that the drummers were playing. Though all of us were extremely tired due to the hard work, no one seemed ready to leave the party and go to sleep yet. We were having too much fun for that.

My vision got blurrier, my senses got hazier as we rocked to the music. And then, there came a time when my body started to protest. I had had too less sleep, too much work and too much alcohol in the past several hours. Not a good combination. My body gave up. I was about to fall.

Just then, I saw a face in front of my eyes. A face which was very, very familiar. Which I had seen thousands of times every day for many, many days.

It was Kanika.

I woke up in Joseph's room to see Thimappa standing in front of me. I looked out of the window. It was dark outside. If I had blacked out at ten in the morning, I must have slept for pretty long. And given the kind of hard work we had done in the past couple of days, I was not surprised.

But as soon as I opened my eyes and registered my surroundings, it hit me. It was Christmas day. There was work to be done. And instead of working, I had carelessly slept all day long.

"Thimappa, I am so sorry. I didn't mean to sleep this long. Is everything okay?" I asked.

"Everything is taken care of, son. We—"

"But the place was a mess—"

"It is all done, Samar. We have done everything. You just concentrate on taking some rest," Thimappa said.

"Okay."

And after giving me a short account of exactly how awesome things had been the previous night, Thimappa left, leaving me alone. I sat there and wondered about it. Wow. The amount we had grossed in the Christmas party was staggering. Even I had not expected the party to be that big a hit. With a smile on my face, I lied down again and tried to sleep. The staff members were capable enough to handle things for one night without my supervision. And Thimappa would definitely come to me if anything went wrong. So, I could sleep some more. But sleep was nowhere to be seen.

I kept lying on the bed for around an hour, but I still couldn't manage to sleep. My eyelids were drooping and my whole body was aching from all that work, but for some reason, I just could not sleep. There was something in the back of my head... something I just could not put a finger on. I stayed within the room all night. I kept feeling a little restless, but still couldn't figure out the reason. I saw my wallet kept on the table. I started fidgeting with it. I came across my college I card in the wallet. And then it struck me. *Kanika*. I had seen Kanika right before I had blanked out.

I had no idea whether I had been hallucinating or it had been real. Either way, it didn't make me happy. I had begun to accept this way of life and had been having a good time there. I had successfully managed not to think of her for so many days. And suddenly, she had made a resounding come back. On top of that, I had to stay indoors and do nothing that night, which made matters only worse.

Unable to stay alone with my thoughts and memories of Kanika, I decided to go for a walk. My eyes kept looking for her. But there was no definite way to confirm, except one. I could go and check the Check In register. That would settle all arguments. I went to the reception and saw the register. Her name was on it. I could understand what had happened. Zeeshan must have told her where I was staying. And she had to meet me and prove her guilt. But how could she deny something I had seen with my own eyes?

I came back to the Village and I decided to go back to work. I went to the area where the party had been held and noticed that it still wasn't set right. So I got down to setting them right. The next thing I knew, the sun was out.

But I still wasn't tired enough to go to sleep. There was no Joseph to force me to keep busy. It is human nature to find rest.

So I decided to go to the beach to take a walk. I had had a peaceful month. Days were zipping by and I liked the clutter in my head. Then why did she have to come and mess everything up? No matter how hard I tried, I could not make my eyes stop looking for her. She had completely overwhelmed my thoughts. She had taken away my mental peace from me.

And then I saw her. In real. She was a few meters away from me. I went past her a couple of times to make sure it really was her, and I wasn't wrong. It was Kanika. She seemed at peace. She was looking at the water and just spending time with herself. The wind was blowing her hair and her eyes were reflecting the twinkle of the morning sun. Her feet were more golden than the sand they were on.

She looked beautiful.

I thought about what I should do next. One option was to just run away. After all, the very purpose of staying back in Goa was to run away from her, wasn't it?

So when she was there, the obvious thing to do would be to run away from her as well. Maybe, I could go back to Delhi even. I didn't necessarily have to go back to the same life. A month in Goa had taught me more than I would have learnt in a year in Delhi. For the time being, I decided to just turn around and go back. I gave her a final glance. And I realized that the thought of just forgiving her was just so tempting.

If only I could forget all about those two minutes of my life, and forgive Kanika and Roy for whatever they had done to me, life would get so much simpler. I would have Kanika by my side again. As I looked at her then, I realized exactly how desperately I wanted that. And that alone was reason enough to make me turn around and rush back to the room.

There was no way I could succumb to the temptation.

24
Was He Better Than Me?

The next day, I was successful in dodging her all day. And it was a difficult task. It was like she was everywhere. Wherever I went, I saw a trace of her. It was getting freakish. But still, I somehow managed not to cross her path. But not for long. In the evening, I found myself face to face with her. It was almost as if she had planned to bump into me. I tried to move past without making second eye-contact, but she did not let me.

"Samar?" she said.

I started to walk away. There was nothing I wanted to say.

"Stop, Samar! At least talk to me once," she called.

I kept walking, without looking back.

Listening to her voice somehow enraged me even more. I felt like breaking a glass or burning some furniture. Maybe I would have, if I had any glass or furniture of my own.

I did not want to spend another second with her. What was there to explain? Why was she even trying? Couldn't she see that she was just hurting me even more? What good would come out of talking about something that can never been undone? The kiss...

Still, when I saw her coming after me, I could not help but want to listen to her. It was still difficult to deny her anything. I was not used to saying no to her. I wanted to listen to her.

And that was what enraged me further. I was angry at myself. All the pain I had gone through to forget about her had gone waste. One moment, out of the blue, she was standing in front of me, pleading me. The way she was looking up at me... I hated myself for denying her what she wanted. But I hated myself more for not wanting to deny her that.

So I walked away, came back to my room and locked it behind me, as if she was chasing me down.

I didn't sleep all day. That happened for the first time since I had come to WoodStock Village. Usually, I was just too tired not to sleep. After trying for hours, tossing and turning in the bed, I knew it was all in vain. At around three in the afternoon, I realized I needed some desperate measures to make me fall asleep.

But I couldn't. So I came out for a walk on the beach.

Kanika occupied my head continuously. When I took a shower, she reminded me of the showers we had taken together. When I walked on the beach, she reminded me of that walk we had taken in the rain. Now that her beautiful face was in front of my eyes, it was even tougher to get her out of my head.

I was standing on the beach that evening. I liked to do that some times. Watching the sun go down into the water. I saw a couple, sitting on the sand. The guy had his arm around the girl and the girl had her head on his shoulder. They seemed deeply in love.

"This is too good to be real," I heard the guy say. I wanted to walk up to him and break his bubble. I wanted to tell him to be careful. Maybe, tell him my story or something. But then, I was never the guy who talked to strangers to deliver unsolicited advice.

I walked on, still looking at the sun. When I got a little tired, I came back to my room, hoping I would be able to sleep.

I reverted to a bottle of rum and switched the lights off. Somehow, I managed to go to sleep.

~

By the time, the New Year Party night came, we had gained enough confidence in ourselves. We knew we could manage any audience. We were better prepared this time. We made better arrangements and handled everything in a better manner. Especially the alcohol. There was no scope for a shortage. Though the night was hard work, it paid off well.

The party was a phenomenal hit. If anything, the turn-up was even larger than that on the Christmas eve. Word travels. And word travels fast. WoodStock Village was getting known.

That day, I had woken up pretty late. Unlike the last day, this time I had no excuse for being lazy or oversleeping. I washed my face immediately and went for a shower. I tried to get back to the party area as soon as I could.

Once I reached the party area, I concentrated single-mindedly to keep myself occupied. And I would have succeeded too, had Kanika not decided to single-mindedly deviate my attention. She kept trying to cross my path as many times as she could. It seemed she was deliberately trying to occupy my mind as much as she could. And she was definitely succeeding in doing so.

After a certain point, I could not take it anymore. Being so near her... loving her so much... hating her so much... it hurt. It was like a constant pain. I physically ached to be with her... talk to her... And holding back was costing me a hell lot more than I could handle.

I was feeling very unsettled. Even in my own domain. It was pretty late. I knew the party would end in less than half an hour. So I decided to run away from the area and go to my half a private place, the kitchen. Thimappa was good company to have. Also, he would keep my head occupied.

I entered with my face hung long.

"All is well?" Thimappa asked.

"Yup. Do you mind if I handle things in the kitchen for a while?" I asked.

"Not at all!"

"Okay. I have explained people what needs to be done outside. I just did not feel like working there today…"

"It's okay. You don't need to justify anything to me. Do what you please," Thimappa laughed.

"Alright. So, I will take over the Pasta for tonight," I said.

"Okay. Take that area, then," he said and pointed one end of the kitchen.

I started making some Pasta and tossed and turned it around more than it was required. It went for quite some while. I let out my anger at my work and it actually helped. By the time I was working on my fourth lot of Pasta for the night, I was feeling considerably better, but not for long.

As I turned to send out the finished dish, it came. The smell. Above the smell of all the things which were being cooked in the kitchen, I smelt a familiar smell. I did not even need to turn around to see who it was. It was Kanika.

I turned around to see her standing close to Thimappa. *Why the fuck could she not leave me alone?* Thimappa looked bemused on seeing her. Never before had a guest come to the kitchen. None as good looking as her, anyway.

"Yes ma'am?" he asked.

"Are you the chef in this place?" she asked.

"Yes."

"I must say I loved the Pasta that I had today!" she said, with excitement. I was pretty sure she was making this up to justify having dropped into the kitchen.

Thimappa's joy knew no bounds. This was a first for him that a beautiful young customer had entered his kitchen to compliment him. It might even have been his dream. The look on his face certainly depicted so.

"Thanks ma'am," he said. "But I am not the one making Pasta. You can thank Samar, there."

I wanted her to disappear from that place that very moment. Instead, she made a beeline to where I was standing. I turned a little away from her.

"Hi," she said when she got to me.

"Hi."

"I loved the Pasta."

"Thanks," I replied shortly.

"I never knew you could cook!"

She was smiling and talking as if nothing wrong had ever happened between the two of us. I couldn't take it. I was fuming.

"And I never knew you kissed my roommates," I reverted.

"Samar—" she started, with hurt evident in her eyes.

"No, Kanika. I'm not listening to anything you have to say. Will you please leave? Do you not fucking understand? I need nothing to do with you. How hard is that to understand? I am in love with someone else. I don't want to be seen with you anymore."

I don't know why I said that. Maybe, I just wanted to see her hurt and offended. I don't know why, but I wanted her to feel a little bit of my pain too. Kanika's face looked as if I had slapped her. She just stared at me. And then, she just turned and left.

But not before I saw tears shining in her eyes. Now what did I do? Wasn't *she* the one who went ahead and cheated? Wasn't *I* the one who was suffering? So why was she crying? I saw her run out of the kitchen and even though I was the one who caused her to cry, I still ached. I could never see her cry. And being a cause of it was unimaginable once... How times change.

Thimappa hadn't heard the conversation between us but he saw her leave with tears in her eyes. He intervened, as soon as she was out of earshot.

"What happened? What did you say to her, Samar?" he cornered me immediately and asked.

"Nothing Thimappa. Please keep out of it."

"Were you hitting on her? Or did you say anything cheap?" he asked.

"What? No. It is nothing to concern you."

Thimappa mumbled something under his breath as he called it a day. He left, cleaning his hands with his apron and the rest of his team left with him. That left me alone.

When I was done with wrapping my work in the kitchen up, I turned to leave, to find Kanika in front of me, once again. I figured that she had just left for a few minutes, until I was alone. But I was in no mood to talk. I said so. "Go away, Kanika. I don't want to talk," I said.

"So will you keep running away from me as long as I am here?"

"If you decide to stay here for long, yes. But it will be great if you just leave."

Kanika paused. I had no idea why she acted so surprised each time I showered my acrimony on her. After what she had done, I was only doing a favour by having not run till then.

"I have come this far to talk to you, Samar. And I will not go without talking to you."

I turned to leave the kitchen.

"Don't I deserve an explanation?" she asked, in a higher volume.

"Explanation? You want an explanation? You kissed my roommate, damn it."

"I kissed him?"

"Yes, I saw that. Roy was all over you with his slimy fingers and kissing you. Don't be so ignorant. I saw what happened, Kanika."

"Are you out of your mind, Samar? I won't ever kiss him. And I didn't. Neither did he!"

"Then what was he doing? Cleaning your lips with his?"

I couldn't have been more acrimonious. Kanika was being hit hard by every sentence that I said. She couldn't take it anymore. She turned around and walked away.

I watched her go. And I realized I couldn't do this anymore. I would have to leave WoodStock to keep my mental peace. The time had come for me to leave.

"I will leave Goa this afternoon," I said to her, from behind.

She turned around and looked at me.

"That is not what I came for. This is your place, Samar. If anybody would have to leave, that will be me. Thank you for knowing me so well."

I nodded. This was what I wanted, at least on the outside. I felt a weird emotion. I had not felt that way ever before. It was an anger of a different level. I felt an urge to harm her. Or maybe hurt her.

"Speak," I said.

"What?"

"I said – speak. You have been saying you wanted to explain since so long. This is your chance. Now, *speak* dammit!" I shouted.

"Okay… See, you will have to trust me when I say this – there is nothing romantic between me and Roy."

"Oh really? So it was just sex? Is that what you mean?"

"No! We never had sex!" she cried out. "Please don't—"

"No sex? Why? Were you guys taking it slow?"

"Shut up! You know it was nothing like that! Why are you doing this? At least let me explain."

"Okay. Explain. That kiss was your first?" I asked, as I tried to stay calm.

"We did not kiss! I told you we never—"

"Then what was it that I saw? *Are you fucking kidding me?*

Do I look like a total moron to you? You think I don't know what a kiss looks like?"

"I... Samar... Will you please calm down?" Kanika said softly, and a little agitated. *Calm down? How was I supposed to?* If I was angry before, my anger had no limits by then. I picked a pan from the slab and threw it on the wall. It made a clamouring sound and fell on the floor. But there was nobody for quite some distance to hear it.

"NO, I *CANNOT* CALM DOWN! You lied to me! You were having an affair behind my back! That too with my own best friend! And now you have the guts to deny that? YOU'VE GOT TO BE FUCKING KIDDING ME!" I thundered.

"Samar—"

"WHAT?"

"I love you..." she whispered, tears flowing down her cheeks.

"THEN TELL ME *WHY?* Why did you go to him? What did I not give you? What was lacking in our relationship?"

"There was nothing lacking! We were perfect!"

"THEN *WHY?*" I shouted.

"Samar..."

And before she could say anymore, I crushed her lips with mine and made her stop. She was taken by surprise at first, but recovered pretty quickly. My mouth came down on her with savage force. I was like a wild animal let loose. I pushed her against the slab of the kitchen. Her weight was on me now. My lips bruised her relentlessly. But she did not seem to mind. In fact, she invited pain. And I gave her that. I tried to pull her tee up but it was just too much hassle. I tore it and threw it away. She pulled me closer. I planted my teeth on her neck and bit her. She let out a cry of pain. The sound of her being in pain made me feel great.

I bit her all over. And asked her, "Was he better than this?"

"Huh?" Kanika said, with a blank expression on her face. She had no idea what had been going on.

"Roy. Was he better than this?"

"*What?* Is that what all this is about?"

"*Just answer my fucking question,*" I shouted.

"Are you insane?"

"Maybe. *Just answer me,*" I gritted my teeth and asked again.

"Go away, Samar Garg. Just leave."

"What do you—?"

"I mean – get out of here! RIGHT NOW," she suddenly shouted.

I stared at her for a second. She was lying topless on the slab. Her torn clothes were lying at a distance. I took off my T-shirt and gave it to her and walked out of the kitchen.

I slammed the door behind me and stood there, listening. After a few seconds, I heard her cry. I walked away.

Sometime later, she told someone from room-service that she would check out that morning. I waited for her to come out of her room with her luggage. When she did, I also noticed the tell-tale signs of tears on her face. I hated myself for making her cry. But it confused me too. Why was *she* crying? Wasn't I the one who lost everything? And what did she want to explain? What was left to explain?

As I saw from a distance, she made her way to the reception to check out. She then called a cab and sat in it. It felt strange to think that she was leaving. Technically, I should have been happy. I was finally getting rid of the negative feeling I got whenever I saw her. But still, I felt a strange emptiness as I saw her sit in the cab. She was close to tears.

Just as the cab was about to leave, another cab stopped alongside. It was Joseph, who had come back from his vacation. He saw that Thimappa was standing at the gate, saying bye to one of the guests. He thought we were being good hosts by saying a personal bye to one of the guests. He started approaching her cab to talk to her.

"I hope you had a good time staying here," he said.

Kanika didn't pay any attention to him. She was too busy being sad about whatever was happening. She looked at him and nodded her head but she couldn't hide the sadness from her eyes. Joseph was taken aback.

"What happened ma'am? Why are you leaving on such a sad note?"

"I just have to go," Kanika said, in the feeblest of voice possible. If I didn't hate her, I would have wanted to hug her. Remember, Joseph didn't hate her.

"I can never let anyone leave WoodStock on such a sad note," he said.

"Honestly, I am okay sir."

"I know you are not okay. And WoodStock is where you have to be," Joseph said, and picked her bags from the cab and brought them out. Kanika looked at him blankly. And then she nodded in affirmation. It was already late in the evening. Joseph asked Kanika to go and sleep but meet him first thing in the morning. I felt a little nervous about all that. Thoughts of running started clouding my mind once again. But it was a place I had begun to love. I did not want to leave it. But I just *had to*.

I decided that my stay at WoodStock was over. I would see Joseph personally as soon as I could and take the next train back.

25

Your Place or Mine?

The next afternoon, as soon as I got up, I went and checked if Kanika and Joseph were talking. They weren't. Around ten minutes later, Kanika walked out of her room and made her way to Joseph's room. I stood in a way, that I could see them but they couldn't see me. They had an intense discussion. I wondered if Kanika told him everything.

When she came out, I could see the tears and the anger in her eyes. Once she was out of sight, I entered Joseph's room to have a talk with him.

"Hi," I said.

"Hey."

"So, how was the vacation?"

"The best time of my life," he smiled and said.

"So what are your plans for business this year?" I asked, to fill some conversation.

"Let's see. I will meet everyone in the evening. The vacation has given me a lot of fresh ideas."

"Great, I will see you then."

"Okay," he said and did not say anything else. He was not going to let away any information, I realized,

"Okay," I said, smiled a fake smile and left.

"What are your plans?"

"I'm going back to Delhi."

"When?"

"Now."

"Okay," Joseph said, as if he knew I would say this.

"Okay?"

"Okay."

Joseph didn't say anything about what he talked with Kanika but I could see that my perception in his eyes had changed a little. I could not tell whether it had changed for the better or for worse. But there was definitely a shift in some way. I wished Navya was still around. Nobody understood me the way she did.

I missed her.

I came out and went straight to my corner of the Village. I didn't have a proper bag, but I had taken polythene bag in which I had once got some vegetables. I stuffed whatever little belongings I had in that and began to exit the Village.

"Where are you going?" I heard Thimappa ask behind me.

"Back."

"Back where?"

"To Delhi," I said.

"What? Don't be so rash, Samar. Think about it," Thimappa said.

"I've thought about it. And I've thought well. There is no way I can stay here any longer," I said.

"But Samar—"

"No! This is it. I'm going. And it's final," I said angrily.

"Let him go," I heard Joseph say.

"What?" Thimappa said. "But—"

"He is only hurting himself. If he is being an idiot, we should let him hurt himself," Joseph said.

"Thanks Joseph," I said.

"Samar?"

"Yes, Joseph?"

"Also, Kanika doesn't want to speak to you anymore."

I heard that and I walked away. I could hear Thimappa and Joseph arguing. It was evident that after my last episode with Kanika, she was pissed at me. Thimappa was trying to help us sort our differences, but she was not willing to talk to me anymore. Suited me. I did not want to talk to her either. I stormed out of WoodStock. I had a few days' salary with me. I took a lift to the railway station. The next thing I knew, I was back on my way to Delhi.

I sat in such a corner that even ticket checker would feel shy about asking me for a ticket. When he finally came, I requested him politely that I didn't have enough money for the tickets. And he didn't really cause any problems after I slipped him some money for his kids.

I was back to sitting alone in the train, with no one to talk to for miles. This is how it had started, possibly from the same train. The last time I had been in it, I was equally dazed and equally angry. The party was now over. It was time to go back to the real thing.

I thought what I would do when I reached Delhi. There was no way I was going back to college. I had a wacky thought. Now that I had worked at WoodStock, I could open my own restaurant in Delhi. I loved the thought, the moment it crossed my mind.

With thoughts of the decor I would keep for my restaurant, I went off to sleep.

26

Broken Soul

I landed in Delhi and it felt strange. I felt as if I was coming back home for the first time. I saw the familiar road and it felt good. I wasn't a foreigner anymore. I didn't have to be curious what I will see round the next corner anymore. I was aware of this place.

I came closer to my college and the weird feeling began to take over. Seeing Kanika's face had given me sleepless nights. But then, I was about to face a bigger challenge. Seeing Roy's face.

I was hoping I would not have to do that, but I also knew that there was possibly no way around the situation because I *had* to go to my flat to pick my stuff.

I reached my flat. The door was locked. I turned around and began to leave. Just as I was leaving, I saw a familiar face. It was Maansi.

"Hey. You're Samar, right?" she asked. It was a little strange that she had to confirm who I was because I had recognized her instantly. But then I realized I looked very different from how she had seen me the last time. My clothes were torn and old and ugly. My skin had tanned in the Goan sun. I looked rugged.

"Hi Maansi," I said, looking down.

"Where have you been, Samar?" she said and took out her

phone from her pocket. She was obviously calling Roy. I slipped past her and left the place.

Once I was out, I thought what to do next. I decided to visit Zeeshan, who lived within walking distance from my flat.

As I walked to his place, I took out the phone from my pocket and turned it on. It was low on battery, which meant I could make only one short call. I called up the only person I had truly missed all this time. Mom.

"Hey Mom," I said, when she picked.

"Samar! Are you alright *beta*? Where have you been? You got us so worried. Your Dad and I were about to leave for Goa tomorrow."

"I had told you I'm okay, Mom. You shouldn't have worried."

"What do you mean you told me? You can't just say that and disappear—"

My phone ran out of battery. I kept it back in my pocket and knocked on Zeeshan's door.

Zeeshan opened the door and gave me a look of disbelief.

"Samar! Where have you been? We were so worried!"

"You, of all the people, shouldn't have been worried Zeeshan. You knew I was in heaven," I said, as he stepped forward and hugged me. It felt good to feel familiar arms around me.

"But why did you have to be such a dick, man? How could you doubt Kanika?"

"I knew what I saw, Zeeshan."

"What? You mean you're still angry with her? Didn't she explain everything in Goa?" he asked.

"What?"

"Wait a minute! Was Kanika able to find you in Goa?"

"Yeah. But we didn't really talk. Why?" I asked.

"Didn't she tell you everything was one big misunderstanding? Oh fuck…"

"I had seen everything with my own eyes, man."

"Sometimes what you see isn't true," Zeeshan said.

"Will you stop giving me fucking *gyaan* and tell me what had happened?" I asked.

"It's not my story to tell you. Let's go to your place. I will ask Roy to come too. He is the right person to tell you everything."

"I will never see Roy again."

"You will have to. I'm not giving you a choice. Come, let's go to your flat," Zeeshan said and called Roy. He told him everything and asked him to come to the flat at the soonest possible.

So we started walking towards my flat. So the moment had finally come when I would be facing Roy. A surge of hatred took over my body. I knew it would be tough to control myself in front of him. What had been happening behind me? What if Kanika and Roy had gotten into a relationship behind me?

When we reached the flat, the door was now open. Roy must have been inside.

I stepped in and saw his face. My blood pressure shot up. I had an instant urge to punch him, but I held it back. He looked at me in a confused way, as if trying to gauge my reaction on seeing him. How could he expect me to be anything but angry?

"Seems like Kanika could not clarify anything?" Roy said, on gauging my reaction.

"What was there to clarify?" I asked. Seriously. What was there to tell? Was I missing something? Everyone seemed to think that if I knew that one thing, everything would fall back in place. What was that all about?

"Oh, so you still don't know?"

"*I don't know what?*" I let out. I'd had enough of it. It was getting on my nerves. I had to know. I had every reason to be shouting.

"That Kanika and I weren't kissing that day," Roy said.

"Shut up, Roy. You think I am blind? You think you both would keep denying the kiss and it would become a fragment of my imagination? Do you think I am that stupid?"

"Listen to me, Samar——"

"No, Roy! *You* listen to *me*! Yes, I might have been stupid enough not to have seen the love brewing between the two of you. But I am not stupid enough to believe you when you say that you were not kissing! *I SAW IT WITH MY OWN FUCKING EYES!*"

"What you saw was *NOT* a kiss," Roy said.

"Oh yes? Then what the fuck *was* it? From where I saw it, it looked damn well like a kiss!"

"WE WERE NOT KISSING, SAMAR! SHE HAD HAD AN ASTHMA ATTACK! AND SHE NEEDED MOUTH TO MOUTH RESPIRATION. I WAS JUST TRYING TO KEEP HER CONSCIOUS UNTIL THE AMBULANCE CAME," Roy shouted.

"What?" I asked. My mind still could not make sense.

"Yes. *That's* what happened," Roy said, getting frenetic.

The images of that fateful day played in front of my eyes. I tried to fit in this explanation for the turn of events. Kanika had not been moving on that day. Roy was on top of her and was doing it rather frantically. When I slammed the door behind me, I just heard Roy's voice shouting 'Samar' but he never came out. Could this have been because he was busy taking care of her as she battled for oxygen? *Fuck.* I could not find a flaw in this explanation. It even explained why Kanika would suddenly go and kiss Roy. It had seemed insane to me all these weeks.

But, again, doubt crept in. Mouth-to-mouth respiration? In an asthma attack? I had researched asthma on the internet pretty well, as Kanika suffered from it, but I did not remember coming across any article that said that mouth-to-mouth resuscitation was given in case of attacks. I turned to Zeeshan, the doctor.

"Does it happen, Zeeshan?"

"Does what happen?" he asked.

"Is mouth-to-mouth respiration given in case of asthma attacks?"

Zeeshan answered my question, but I stopped listening after the first word. "Yes. In some cases, when the attack is..."

My first reaction was elation. My Kanika had not been an infidel after all. The incident had shaken up everything I had ever believed in simply because I had started believing that my judgment was good for nothing. But then I realized what an idiot I had been. Not because I had been angry all this time. But because I had not given Kanika even a single chance to talk to me in Goa.

I wanted to look for her immediately. I needed to talk to her and get everything sorted. If she was still willing to talk to me. Man, I had been such a fool. I doubted her and left the city. And when she came back to try and explain things to me, I hurt her repeatedly. I did not give her a chance to explain. Instead I hurt her deliberately, sadistically. I then saw how mean I had been with her. How crushed she must have been. I felt extremely guilty. I hated myself for doing what I did to her. It was unforgivable.

Still, I hoped she would forgive me...

I turned to look at Roy. That was the first time that I realised that he had been talking non-stop to me. Explaining things. How Kanika's health had suddenly gotten worse. How that kiss... no mouth-to-mouth respiration happened. How shattered she was after I left. How her health had gone worse.

They had called me frantically, once she was out of danger. But it was already too late. I had switched my phone off by then. And they had no idea where I was. Until Roy bumped into Zeeshan one day. Zeeshan asked Roy if I was back from Goa yet. And that was how Roy got to know that I was in Goa.

Once Kanika was in a good enough condition to travel, she

had come rushing to Goa. To explain things, to get back together. But I had not given her a chance. I had hurt her again and again, throwing unjustifiable jibes at her at every chance I got. And then I had come back. They had been calling me from Goa, unceasingly for the past three days. And I had been ignoring all the calls.

I felt like shit. Wasn't I supposed to take care of her forever? So why did I turn into the cause of all her pain... all the tears...?

I had to talk to her. I needed to apologize. Properly. Maybe I would think of something grand. Some kind of surprise that she would love...

But first things first. I had to apologize to Roy first. I turned to him, but he motioned me to stop by holding his palm up.

"Save it."

"But I... I'm really sorry, Roy..."

"I know," he laughed. "But please don't apologize, man! I understand how it must have looked to you. The overreaction was unnecessary, but you came around! Better late than never."

"I was such a fool... If only I had just listened..." I shook my head at my stupidity.

"It's okay, man. She loves you. She would understand," Roy said.

"Yes," I nodded. "I would do anything to win her back."

"So what are you waiting for?"

"What if... what if she doesn't agree to speak to me?" I asked.

"Then we would run to Goa and bug her incessantly till she agrees!"

I laughed and took my phone out to call her. But the call went unanswered. I called her again. Again, no response. I tried calling her several times but nobody picked up.

"Don't worry. Why don't you just reach Goa tomorrow morning and apologize personally?" Zeeshan suggested.

I liked the idea. She would be easier to control in person.

On the phone, she would be rather tough to manage.

"Okay, if you say so," I said, and forced a smile.

"Yeah man. That's the spirit. Now tell me, what will you have tonight? Old Monk or Whisky?"

"Old Monk."

In spite of sleeping late, I got up early. Zeeshan was sleeping next to me. In the other room, Roy and Maansi were fast asleep. In the time that I had been in Goa, Maansi had realized that she could not live without Roy. She loved him too much to stay away. So she had gone back to him and they got back together. They were very much in love and it showed.

I filled in some stuff in my bag and prepared to leave. I found my wallet in my room. If only I had my ATM card when I was in Goa, life could have been very different there. But maybe, not having money in Goa was the best thing about the whole trip.

I picked my bag and left for the airport. I resisted the urge to call her, as I called the Customer Care to ask at what time the first flight to Goa was. By noon, I was in Goa. I took a cab to WoodStock. I was going there dressed in a very different way today. I was looking forward to meeting everyone else as well, even thought it had just been three days since I had met them.

I reached WoodStock and looked for Kanika. Her room was locked, so I started looking for Joseph. He was nowhere as well.

I called up Kanika's phone number but nobody picked it.

"Where is Joseph?" I asked a local guy who worked there.

"He has gone to the doctor with a guest. The girl who lived there," the guy said and pointed to the same *hut where Kanika had been living.*

Kanika was unwell. I felt a little unsettled about everything. I needed to know immediately what was happening. I rushed to the local clinic. There was not even a proper hospital in Arambol. I was worried about the type of care Kanika must have been getting.

When I got to the clinic, I saw Joseph standing outside. He wasn't as surprised on seeing me, as I was expecting him to be.

"So you didn't go or you went and came back?" he asked on seeing me, without any pleasantries.

"I came back. Is she unwell?"

"Yes. Very."

"What happened? Is she okay?" I asked, a little frantic by then.

"She is a little serious. She had a terrible asthma attack. The doctor is trying his best but he doesn't have enough equipment."

"And why are there no hospitals in Arambol?"

"I know this place needs one. But the doctor is trying his best," Joseph said sombrely.

I walked inside the clinic. The doctor was in the other room with Kanika. I walked into the room, without asking anyone. I saw the scene. I don't know much about the medical field, but I could clearly see that the doctor was struggling with his broken down, old equipment. The moment I saw him, I knew we needed to move Kanika from there.

I came out and told Joseph that we needed to shift her to Panjim, the capital city of Goa, which was supposed to have the best medical facilities. He agreed.

We talked to the doctor and told him we wanted to shift her.

"But she is too critical to be shifted at this stage. You should wait till tomorrow. If she improves, you can shift her."

I had no idea what was happening. How could this happen? This is what my life had become. Every time I felt everything is going to fall in place, something drastic happened. No Kanika. No. You can't leave me, I chanted in my head.

In the evening, I sent Joseph home, as I sat on the waiting bench outside. I looked at Kanika through the glass in the door. She looked angelic, lying on the bed. I came back to the bench and dialled Mr Vinod Merchant's number. Kanika's dad. I had come to know him pretty well the previous year when I had met him at Kanika's place.

"Hello uncle."

"Hi. Samar, right? How're you, son?" Mr Merchant said.

"I'm okay, uncle. How are you?"

"I'm good. How is Kanika? Were you two able to solve the problems between the two of you? Kanika didn't tell me much about it... just that there was some misunderstanding...?"

"Actually, uncle..." I began to speak.

"Yes, *beta?*"

"Kanika is unwell."

"What? What happened to her?" he asked, suddenly sounding very alert.

"Her asthma is acting really badly. Her lungs have got really weak. She's in the hospital and she is quite critical."

"Oh my God. What... When did this happen?"

"I got to know about it just today, uncle, after I got to Goa..." I explained.

"What? Goa? What are you talking about? What are you doing in Goa?"

"Uncle, I came here to meet Kanika, and clear our misunderstanding—"

"But in Goa? What was Kanika doing there?" Mr Merchant asked.

"She came to talk to me, to solve the misunderstanding between us..."

"You are not making any sense to me at all."

"I mean—" I started, but he cut me off mid-sentence.

"Never mind. We can talk about that later. Just tell me – where is Kanika right now?"

"She's here at Goa. She's admitted to a clinic for treatment."

"Clinic? But you said her condition was serious! Why isn't she in a hospital?" Mr Merchant sounded very panicked by then.

"That's because there is no proper hospital here, at Arambol village. We have decided of shifting her to Panjim..."

"Panjim? Isn't she well enough to come to Delhi?"

"No uncle. We have to get her treated here," I replied.

"I'll be there as quickly as possible."

"But uncle, her condition is really critical... we have to shift her as soon as possible... But the doctors have asked us to wait another day, to see if she is in a condition to be moved..."

"Okay, I understand... I'll be there as soon as I can," he said and hung up.

I could sense the fear in his voice. It would be better to have some support to handle this situation. I needed a hand. As I lied down on the uncomfortable bench, I thought of every second I had spent with Kanika. Expectedly, there was no way I could go to sleep.

The next morning, the doctor was scheduled to come at nine in the morning. Mr Merchant had left Delhi, but would not be reaching before noon. I was feeling a little uneasy about having to make some big decision alone, without consulting anyone.

Thankfully, Joseph reached the Hospital at quarter to nine. And we started waiting for the doctor.

The doctor was fifteen minutes late. He asked us to wait outside, as he went inside and carried out his checks, as Joseph and I waited outside Kanika's room.

When he came out, the doctor looked really tensed, which made my heart sink.

"Yes, doctor?"

"She's still quite critical. And I'm afraid – we don't have the equipment to do anything."

"Can we take her to Panjim?" I asked.

"That will be very risky."

"So, what should we do?"

"Keeping her here will also not help. I guess, taking her to Panjim is a risk we might have to take," the doctor suggested.

"But doctor, what if…?" Joseph began to ask, but trailed away.

The doctor looked at him and gave him a worried look. That only meant one thing. That it was dangerous to take her to Panjim, but it was a risk we would have to take because she was not getting any better living here. My heart sank.

"When should we do it?" Joseph asked.

"As soon as possible."

"Can we wait till noon? Her father will be reaching then," I said.

"I don't think that will benefit us in any way. It can only make matters worse," the doc said.

"So, should we do it right now?"

"I will ask the nurse to start making the preparations. I will also arrange an ambulance."

"Thanks doctor."

The doctor left. I had a terrible feeling in my chest. I had never felt so low. I called up Mr Merchant, but his phone was not reachable. A part of me was dying every passing second.

A little while later, I saw the nurse push Kanika's bed into the ambulance. I sat beside her, holding her hand. She was unconscious, with an oxygen mask on her face.

I looked at her face. Her expression was contorted. It seemed as if she was in pain. I got even more worried. If only she would just open her eyes for a minute to look at me... I would have told her how sorry I was. I would have told her how deeply I regretted the pain that I made her go through all this while.

I would have asked her for forgiveness. But most of all, I would have asked her to come back. To never close her eyes again, and to never be sick again. I would have asked her to fight her ailment, and to come back to where I was waiting for her... with all the love she deserved. All the love that she had asked for, and I had denied her...

If only she would give me a chance.

I would die if she left me. There was no way I was strong enough to live without her. I wanted her back. I needed her in my life.

"Hey Ram, hey Ram," I was enchanting inside my head. I was normally not religious. But such moments can make anyone religious. If it could improve her chances of survival by half a percent, I would take it. My eyes wanted to cry. But this was not the time. I had to be strong and fight it out.

The road was bumpy and the ambulance was moving fast. Kanika was completely immobile. I had no indicator to know that she was alright. I sat through nervously for twenty minutes, until the ambulance reached a hospital in Panjim. Once we got there, the ambulance came to a stop. I held Kanika's stretcher to prevent any harm to her.

The doors of the ambulance opened and I saw the man who had been driving, come in. The clinics at Arambol were short of staff. They moved Kanika's stretcher and shifted her to a room and the doctors came rushing. He walked in and checked Kanika's pulse. He looked at me with horror.

My heart beat froze.

For three complete seconds, I was completely immobile. And then I heard voices around me. There were nurses and compounders coming towards us, talking quickly, and discussing their strategy for their new patient. Kanika.

"Get her inside... Now!"

"To the ICU. Call Dr Ranjit..."

"Clear the way..."

I heard them speak, but I did not look at them. I never broke eye-contact from the doctor who had first rushed to take Kanika's pulse. I wanted to know what was wrong. Why had he looked so worried?

But soon, Kanika was taken inside the ICU and I heard noises from inside. They were frantic. It was not a good sign. I was very scared. My blood turned cold and my knees gave out. I took support from the wall, as I breathed heavily and tried to relax.

It isn't over yet. It isn't over yet, I tried to tell myself.

Ten agonizing minutes later, minutes that felt like decades, the doctors finally came out. The expressions on their faces said it all. I knew that very moment what they were saying with their eyes.

Kanika was no more.

She had left us. I collapsed that very moment. All the blood in my body had been sucked out. I didn't have any energy. I looked at Joseph. He was close to tears. I felt everything around me fading. I somehow managed to gather myself and saved myself from collapsing.

I took a chair nearby and held my head in my hands. Just then, my phone rang. It was Roy.

"Hello?" he said, as I received the call. I let out a loud crying wail.

"What happened, Samar?"

"Roy..." I couldn't stop crying.

"Yes, Samar? Tell me what happened?"

"Something terrible has happened, Roy."

"Tell me what it is, man! You're killing me here," he shouted.

"Something... something bad has happened... come soon to Goa..."

"What is it? Just tell me, dammit!"

"Samar, Kanika... Kanika... I can't say it..." I stammered, crying louder now.

"Kanika *what?* What happened to her? Is she okay?"

"No, she is not... Her asthma..."

"Her asthma? Is it giving her trouble again?" he asked. "Is she okay? Is that why you haven't been taking my calls since you left?"

"I... I could not..."

"I am coming, Samar. I'm taking the first flight out."

"Roy... Kanika is no more..." I said, finally.

"*What?* I... No! This can't be... this can't be," Roy whispered, more to himself.

I cut the call and went inside the ICU to look at Kanika, lying peacefully in front of me. I had seen her sleep. She looked just the same. How could such a terrible thing possibly happen?

My world came crashing down around me. This could not be true. This just could not be true. My Kanika... My baby... She was no more... She left me, forever... I could not think. As the sobs shook my body, all I could do was tremble. Her thoughts, her memories kept flooding my head. I had gone numb. All I saw was her pretty face, looking at me with love, telling me how much she loved me. Her sweet smile when I told her how lucky I was to have her. Her innocent eyes, as she met mine and asked me how much I loved her...

Every second spent with her flashed before my eyes. Each memory more painful than the last. I had promised I would be with her forever. That I would never let her go. But I had... I had left her alone at the worst phase of her life. When she was battling that horrific ailment, I had not been with her. Every day, she had died little by little... more because of me, less because of the disease.

But she got her revenge! I left her alone for a while... and in turn, she left me alone forever. That was not fair. That was so not fair. She had never harmed anyone in her life. Then why did life have to be so brutal with her? Why her? Why my baby?

How could I? Kanika died. She was no more. I could not even get a chance to tell her how much I loved her. Some more tears came. It was not like I did not get a chance to tell her... I got plenty. But I did not want to. I hated her for doing something she never did. And I never gave her a chance to explain. How could I ever doubt her? How could I ever even think that she was unfaithful? She was so sweet, she would never even have so much as looked at any other guy. She loved me. And only me. And all I did was hurt her. That was how I paid back for all her love. By killing her... with my words... with my aloofness... with that revengeful kiss... I hated myself. I felt like dying. I did not deserve to live. I was the one person she trusted in the world, and I had been so cruel to her.

And she left me. That was her revenge. It was as if her death was not caused by asthma, but it was I who killed her... slowly... every day.

I was a murderer.

Meanwhile, Mr Merchant arrived. He was in complete denial for the first five minutes. He just couldn't process what he was seeing. Everything had been sudden for me but it was even more sudden for him.

It took a while to sink into him but when it did, he was a mess.

I could not handle my own pain. To even think of what he must have been going through was unbearable. I could not take it.

I left the room. Joseph was going to take over from there.

He talked to the doctor and got a handle on the situation. Mr Merchant and I were way too unstable. Mr Merchant was still with Kanika, inside the room when I came out.

"I will see you at WoodStock," I said to Joseph, as I was crossing him.

I came back to WoodStock and went to the same corner where I had stayed all those days. I made sure I didn't bump into anyone. I just found my corner and sat there silently, lost in my thoughts.

A few hours later, I got out of my meditative state. I got up from there and came to the open area of WoodStock. I was taken aback by what I saw.

Kanika's last rituals seemed to have started there. Her body was lying in the middle and Mr Merchant, Thimappa and Joseph were sitting there, along with some other people.

I walked up to them, and silently went and sat beside Joseph.

He saw me and said, "Mr Merchant wants the ritual to take place in Goa itself."

I nodded.

No one made a sound. And then, I saw her. There, lying in the middle, wrapped in plain white clothes, was Kanika. Dead. I went to her... She was looking beautiful. At peace. Had she forgiven me? For killing her? For leaving her alone? For making her face all that I had made her?

Would I ever be able to erase the picture of her lying dead from my memory? No. I knew that would never happen. I touched her cheek. She did not look dead. It was as if she were sleeping. As if she would wake up any moment. She would open her eyes and turn to me, like she used to do... she would hold my gaze and smile sweetly... and whisper in my ears... that she loved me.

And I would tell her that I loved her too. But she would not listen. She would never listen. And then came the pain... and never left.

The incident had broken more than one person. I would never be the same person again. Mr Merchant would never be the same person again. Roy would never be the same person again. We were now broken souls, living an incomplete life.

However, life goes on. Everybody moves on. We came back to WoodStock after the rituals in the cremation grounds. Joseph disappeared in his room. And Mr Merchant and I were sitting in the open area with Thimappa. Nobody was speaking. Each one of us was just lost in his own thoughts.

"What happened, Thimappa? Tell me what exactly happened," I finally broke the silence.

Thimappa took a deep breath. He knew this was going to be difficult. But then, it had to be done. We needed to know how and what had happened. I put my hand on my face and heard in deep concentration, as Thimappa prepared to narrate the most tragic day of my life.

Kanika took a shower that day. She was really depressed. She had cried all night and her heart wasn't behaving too well either. Thimappa didn't know the cause, but as she sat alone in her room, something triggered an asthma attack. She was choking and she needed medical attention immediately. She somehow managed to stumble out of her room, where around ten minutes later, a tourist spotted her lying outside her room.

The tourist called Joseph, who called Thimappa. Together, they lifted her and transferred her to a car and took her to the nearby dispensary. She wasn't moving and from what Thimappa could tell, possibly wasn't breathing either. By the time they reached the clinic, the doctor told them that she was critical.

Joseph and Thimappa had no clue what to do. She had not given any phone numbers in the entry register. And I had not been taking any calls from any Goa number. So as she lay in the clinic, they just sat and prayed for us to contact them.

I reached the next day.

What I had done... It was one big mistake. And an irreversible one at that. I had no idea how I was going to live the rest of my life with this guilt on my back. But I would have to. There was no other option.

Mr Merchant had a small tear in his right eye. I was half shaking. It was a difficult story to hear. I was messed up. I did not know where to look, what to do next, how to tell everyone, how to react, how to control myself or how to comfort the father sitting in front of me. But I decided to be selfish. I realized that my first priority was to handle myself. The last thing I wanted to add to Mr Merchant's worries was to comfort me.

I walked to the beach, alone and looked at the horizon. And thought of all the years in front of me. I thought of waking up every day, knowing that I was responsible for everything. If only, I had heard her out, things could have been different. If only, I had let her tell me that she loved me.

27

I will never forget that day

7th April. The day she decided to leave us all. It's been a few years, but whenever I think of that day, something around my spine and in the pit of my stomach, shifts its place a little bit. And for what? For a stupid misunderstanding which shouldn't have happened at all. What had happened had left a scar... that would never fade. I would always love her... I would always miss her.

There had not been a day since she left that I had not thought about her and felt hurt. It was a physical ache. I dealt with it every day... day after day... And it was getting better. Time does lessen the pain. But it never goes. It's always there. I try to run from it and I am successful at times... but never completely. The more I laugh in the day, the harder I cry at night.

Happens every time.

It's a very personal chapter of my life and it feels really weird to be sharing it. It is like baring naked in front of public about my deepest emotions. She is gone. She isn't living through the agony. Leaving all of us behind. Most lives moved on unchanged. But two lives changed completely when she left.

The first one was mine. I couldn't see or think about anything the way I earlier had. I became way too serious. I missed the lighter side of everything I saw. And the second one was of

Kanika's father. With both – his wife and his daughter – not in this world, every night was going to be a struggle for him. I try my best to be with him and see through his pain. I owe Kanika that much.

And that is the least I could do for him for taking his daughter's life. I still feel like a murderer. The incident has shaped me the way I am today. Roy says that this is probably why I got into writing in the first place. But he never believed I could actually write down such an honest account of the whole episode. I know he won't believe me until he actually sees this in print.

I am often asked – *Do you still miss her?* The answer, of course, is *yes*. I can never stop missing her. I have definitely moved on in life, but that doesn't mean I stopped missing her. Some other people ask me – *Do you cry yourself to bed?* The answer to this one is no. Because I don't see a point in crying. The important thing is that her thought is in my heart. And that is how I want to keep it. I have never been a crying person.

Except some nights, when the pain gets just way too unbearable.

It's easier in the day, when I can keep myself occupied. It's the night time which kills me. Some days are better, while some are worse. I try my best to occupy myself with something or the other.

I had several cycles.

Dark circles. Insomnia. Blood Pressure. Headaches. I saw it all. And you know, headaches and insomnia aren't good together. They're like a circle – I don't sleep, my head aches. My head aches, I don't sleep... It just keeps going on.

I even took some drugs once. Don't freak out. They were not that bad and I took them for like ten days for a month. But I soon stopped. It's not that bad for one time use. And I took it on prescription. I went through the entire process of meeting the doctor and everything.

Today, I have managed to start thinking of other things. I have moved on. But every time someone mentions Goa, my thoughts go back to that same day. I see her, wrapped in that white cloth, flowers all over her. Cotton balls stuffed in her nose.

I see those four people lift her body. I see everyone cry. I see the crowd that had gathered at her place. Her entire family and circle of friends was there.

When I lost her, I lost everything. My best friend. Someone who'd listen to all kinds of bullshit I had to say. Who'd look up to me even after seeing me at my worst. Who'd love me unconditionally. Who'd care the most. Who'd be there when I need someone. Who'd miss me. Who'd think I am the smartest guy on the planet. Who'd click shitloads of pictures of me, dressing me up in stupid clothes. Who'd tell about me to her friends, very proudly. Whose female friends would fall in love with me, just by hearing my description from her. Who'd be my partner in crime. Who'd dance with me to the tune of old Hindi songs in the middle of the night. Who'd call at the middle of the night, talking about some stupid reality show on TV. Who'd go to shopping with me, whenever and wherever. Who I can force my choices on. Who'd ask me to like all her pictures on FB.

I miss her very, very much.

Though life moves on and we move on with it, some things stay. The pain stays. It's with me, always. I have to deal with it every day. I just hope that wherever she is, she is happy. At least happier than the hell I made her go through in the last moments of her life.

I would never forgive myself.

I just wish she would. Especially because I had promised her that I will never let her go.

Epilogue

I was sitting with Arshi and Mom in the living room. I had been telling them the story for the past six hours. Arshi was a good listener. At times, a tear or two had managed to escape her eyes, but she did not drop her psychologist's cap at any time.

"It will be okay *beta*. Time heals all wounds," Mom said to me. She had used the same line at least a thousand times on me. It was as ineffective as it had been every time.

"So, what do you think?" Mom asked Arshi.

"I don't have much to say," Arshi said. "I'm a little too overwhelmed to say anything."

"It's okay… Take your time…" Mom said.

"Can I leave?" I asked. I wanted to go back to my room, my area of comfort. I needed some time to myself. Somehow, I wasn't comfortable being around anyone for so long.

"Okay, *beta*," Mom said.

I got up and left for my room. And as soon as I closed the door behind me, I put an ear on the door to hear what the ladies were talking about.

"So… what do you think? Would he be okay?" Mom asked Arshi.

"Aunty, Samar is undergoing a very deep state of depression. But I don't think we should put him on medication. I think he needs to come out of it himself."

"We have tried everything. We just don't know what to do now."

"Even I'm clueless… I will think of something and call you when I get some idea," Arshi reassured Mom.

"Okay *beta*. I'll be waiting for your call."

"Okay Aunty. I should go now…" I heard her say as she got up from her seat. "Did you get in touch with that girl Navya?"

"No. Actually, I got to know about her just today, as he was telling the story. Why?"

"Did you see the look in his eyes when he was talking about her?"

"Yes. He seemed to like her a lot at a point in time," Mom said.

"Yeah. You think we should call her?" Arshi asked.

"Oh God. Definitely! But how do we get her number?"

"We can ask Joseph. Maybe he can arrange something. You have Joseph's number?"

"Yeah. I do. Why don't you call him? And ask him to find out Navya's number?" Mom suggested.

"Okay, Aunty."

Arshi called Joseph and explained everything to him. I heard her take a number from him and write it down.

"Joseph has checked his record. This is Navya's number in Bhopal."

"Okay. Call then."

Arshi dialled the number and put her phone on loudspeaker.

The Vodafone number you're trying to call, is presently not in use.

Jis Vodafone number pe, aap sampark karna chaahte, woh abhi service me nahi hai.

Author's Note

On that note, I wish to end this book. This is big enough a share of my life for now. I'm sure you want to know what happened after.

Many people write about one or two incidents of their lives. But this time, I am writing about THE incident, which kind of shaped everything around me and everything about me. It tells you who I am and why I am who I am.

We all remember certain episodes in our lives where we have been kiddish. Also, we have all had a phase where we were more carefree than ever after. We all relish those days. But then, in some cases, things happen which makes us leave that carefree attitude behind, and get mature sooner that we would wish.

People say I am more serious than others. People meet me and tell me, I am a little different. I often sit and wonder why it is so. Maybe after reading the book you would be able to tell me why. The biggest favour you can do me is to mail me and tell me what you think.

This book chronicles why I became a writer in the first place. What happened and what that lead to, which brought us here, on this crossroad, where I am writing and you are actively interested in reading what I am writing. That's why, it will always remain special.

At that time, it had seemed like the end of the world. I thought I would never be able to be a normal person ever again. But then, such is human life. It fights back whenever you stop giving it a chance.

I write stories based one year of my life. The book 'It's First Love… just like the last one!' was based on the twentieth year of my life. 'Never Let Me Go…' is about the twenty first year.

Definitely, I will document the following year very soon, hopefully, by July, 2012. This was the story of the twenty first year of my life. That will be the story of the twenty second year of my life.

I hope you will read that one too. And tell me what you thought.

What did this incident lead me to?

Where did I land up?

How did life shape?